LUKE WALTON

BY

HORATIO ALGER, Jr.

uthor of "Bound to Rise," "Jack's Ward," "Making
His Way," etc.

WILDSIDE PRESS

CONTENTS

iii

CONTENTS

LUKE WALTON

CHAPTER I

A CHICAGO NEWSBOY

"*News* and *Mail*, one cent each!"

Half a dozen Chicago newsboys, varying in age from ten to sixteen years, with piles of papers in their hands, joined in the chorus.

They were standing in front and at the sides of the Sherman House, on the corner of Clark and Randolph Streets, one of the noted buildings in the Lake City. On the opposite side of Randolph Street stands a massive but somewhat gloomy stone structure, the Court House and City Hall. In the shadow of these buildings, at the corner, Luke Walton, one of the largest newsboys, had posted himself. There was something about his bearing and appearance which distinguished him in a noticeable way from his companions.

To begin with, he looked out of place. He was well grown, with a frank, handsome face, and was better dressed than the average newsboy. That was one reason, perhaps, why he preferred to be by himself, rather than to engage in the scramble for customers which was the habit of the boys around him.

It was half-past five. The numerous cars that passed were full of business men, clerks, and boys, returning to their homes after a busy day.

Luke had but two papers left, and he was anxious to dispose of them so that he, too, might go home. But these two for some unaccountable reason remained on his hands an unusual length of time. But at length a comfortable-looking gentleman of middle age, coming from the direction of La Salle Street, paused and said, " You may give me a *News*, my boy."

Luke gladly complied with the request.

" Here you are, sir," he said, briskly.

The gentleman took the paper, and thrusting his hand into his pocket, began to feel for a penny, but apparently without success.

" I declare," he said, smiling, " I believe I am penniless. I have nothing but a five-dollar bill."

" Never mind, sir! Take the paper and pay me to-morrow."

" But I may not see you."

" I am generally here about this time."

" And if I shouldn't see you, you will lose the penny."

" I will risk it, sir," said Luke, smiling.

" You appear to have confidence in me."

" Yes, sir."

"Then it is only fair that I should have confidence in you."

Luke looked puzzled, for he didn't quite understand what was in the gentleman's mind.

"I will take both of your papers. Here is a five-dollar bill. You may bring me the change to-morrow, at my office, No. 155 La Salle Street. My name is Benjamin Afton."

"But, sir," objected Luke, "there is no occasion for this. It is much better that I should trust you for two cents than that you should trust me with five dollars."

"Probably the two cents are as important to you as five dollars to me. At any rate, it is a matter of confidence, and I am quite willing to trust you."

"Thank you, sir, but——"

"I shall have to leave you, or I shall be home late to dinner."

Before Luke had a chance to protest further, he found himself alone, his stock of papers exhausted, and a five-dollar bill in his hand.

While he stood on the corner in some perplexity, a newsboy crossed Randolph Street, and accosted him.

"My eyes, if you ain't in luck, Luke Walton," he said. "Where did you get that bill? Is it a one?"

"No, it's a five."

"Where'd you get it?"

"A gentleman just bought two papers of me."

"And gave you five dol .rs! You don't expect me to swaller all that, do y(￼?"

"I'm to bring him the c ￼nge to-morrow," continued Luke.

The other boy nearly doubled up with merriment.

"Wasn't he jolly green, though?" he ejaculated.

"Why was he?" asked Luke, who by this time felt considerably annoyed.

"He'll have to whistle for his money."

"Why will he?"

"'Cause he will."

"He won't do anything of the sort. I shall take him his change to-morrow morning."

"What?" ejaculated Tom Brooks in a shrill crescendo.

"I shall carry him his change in the morning—four dollars and ninety-eight cents. Can't you understand that?"

"You ain't going to be such a fool, Luke Walton?"

"If it's being a fool to be honest, then I'm going to be that kind of a fool. Wouldn't you do the same?"

"No, I wouldn't. I'd just invite all the boys round the corner to go with me to the theayter. Come, Luke, be a good feller, and give us all a blowout. We'll go to the theayter, and afterwards we'll have an oyster stew. I know a bully place on Clark Street, near Monroe."

" Do you take me for a thief, Tom Brooks? " exclaimed Luke, indignantly.

" The gentleman meant you to have the money. Of course he knew you wouldn't bring it back. Lemme see, there's a good play on to Hooley's. Six of us will cost a dollar and a half, and the oyster stews will be fifteen cents apiece. That'll only take half the money, and you'll have half left for yourself."

" I am ashamed of you, Tom Brooks. You want me to become a thief, and it is very evident what you would do if you were in my place. What would the gentleman think of me? "

" He don't know you. You can go on State Street to sell papers, so he won't see you."

" Suppose he should see me? "

" You can tell him you lost the money. You ain't smart, Luke Walton, or you'd know how to manage."

" No, I am not smart in that way, I confess. I shan't waste any more time talking to you. I'm going home."

" I know what you are going to do. You're goin' to spend all the money on yourself."

" Don't you believe that I mean to return the change? "

" No, I don't."

" I ought not to complain of that. You merely credit me with acting as you would act yourself. How many papers have you got left? "

" Eight."

" Here, give me half, and I will sell them for you, that is, if I can do it in fifteen minutes."

" I'd rather you'd take me to the theayter," grumbled Tom.

" I have already told you I won't do it."

In ten minutes Luke had sold his extra supply of papers, and handed the money to Tom. Tom thanked him in an ungracious sort of way, and Luke started for home.

It was a long walk, for the poor cannot afford to pick and choose their localities. Luke took his way through Clark Street to the river, and then, turning in a northwesterly direction, reached Milwaukee Avenue. This is not a fashionable locality, and the side streets are tenanted by those who are poor or of limited means.

Luke paused in front of a three-story frame house in Green Street, which might have been improved by a coat of paint. He ascended the steps and opened the door, for this was the newsboy's home.

CHAPTER II

A LETTER FROM THE DEAD

In the entry Luke met a girl of fourteen with fiery red hair, which apparently was a stranger to the comb and brush. She was the landlady's daughter, and, though of rather fitful and uncertain temper, always had a smile and pleasant word for Luke, who was a favorite of hers.

" Well, Nancy, how's mother? " asked the newsboy, as he began to ascend the front stairs.

" She seems rather upset like, Luke," answered Nancy.

" What has happened to upset her? " asked Luke, anxiously.

" I think it's a letter she got about noon. It was a queer letter, all marked up, as if it had been travelin' round, and was stained with tobacco. How it did smell! I took it in myself, and carried it up to your ma. I stayed to see her open it, for I was kind of curious to know who writ it."

" Well? "

" As soon as you ma opened it, she turned as pale as ashes, and I thought she'd faint away. She put her hand on her heart just so," and Nancy placed

7

a rather dirty hand of her own, on which glittered a
five-cent brass ring, over that portion of her anat-
omy where she supposed her heart lay.

" She didn't faint away, did she? " asked Luke,
quickly.

" No, not quite.".

" Did she say who the letter was from? "

" No; I asked her, but she said, ' From no one
that you ever saw, Nancy.' I say, Luke, if you find
out who's it from, let me know. I shan't sleep a
wink if I don't find out."

" I won't promise, Nancy. Perhaps mother would
prefer to keep it a secret."

" Oh, well, keep your old secrets, if you want to,"
said Nancy, pettishly.

" Don't be angry, Nancy; I will tell you if I can,"
and Luke hurried upstairs to the third story, which
contained the three rooms occupied by his mother,
his little brother, and himself.

Opening the door, he saw his mother sitting in a
rocking-chair, apparently in deep thought, for the
work had fallen from her hands and lay in her lap.
There was an expression of sadness in her face, as
if she had been thinking of the happy past, when
the little family was prosperous, and undisturbed by
poverty or privation.

" What's the matter, mother? " asked Luke, with
solicitude.

Mrs. Walton looked up quickly.

" I have been longing to have you come back,

Luke," she said. "Something strange has happened to-day."

"You received a letter, did you not?"

"Who told you, Luke?"

"Nancy. I met her as I came in. She said she brought up the letter, and that you appeared very much agitated when you opened it."

"It is true."

"From whom was the letter, then, mother?"

"From your father."

"What!" exclaimed Luke, with a start. "Is he not dead?"

"The letter was written a year ago."

"Why, then, has it arrived so late?"

"Your father on his deathbed intrusted it to some-one who mislaid it, and has only just discovered and mailed it. On the envelope he explains this, and expresses his regret. It was at first mailed to our old home, and has been forwarded from there. But that is not all, Luke. I learn from the letter that we have been cruelly wronged. Your father, when he knew he could not live, intrusted to a man in whom he had confidence, ten thousand dollars to be conveyed to us. This wicked man could not resist the temptation, but kept it, thinking we should never know anything about it. You will find it all explained in the letter."

"Let me read it, mother," said Luke, in excitement.

Mrs. Walton opened a drawer of the bureau, and

placed in her son's hands an envelope, brown and
soiled by contact with tobacco. It was directed to
her in a shaky hand. Across one end were written
these words:

"This letter was mislaid. I have just discovered
it, and mail it, hoping it will reach you without
further delay. Many apologies and regrets.

"J. HANSHAW."

Luke did not spend much time upon the envelope,
but opened the letter.

The sight of his father's familiar handwriting
brought the tears to his eyes, moving him, though
not in the same degree as it had moved his mother.
This was the letter:

"GOLD GULCH, California.

"MY DEAR WIFE: It is a solemn thought to me
that when you receive this letter these trembling
fingers will be cold in death. Yes, dear Mary, I
know very well that I am on my deathbed, and
shall never more be permitted to see your sweet
face, or meet again the gaze of my dear children.
Last week I contracted a severe cold while mining,
partly through imprudent exposure; and have
grown steadily worse, till the doctor, whom I summoned from Sacramento, informs me that there is
no hope, and that my life is not likely to extend
beyond two days.

" This is a sad end to my dreams of future happiness with my little family gathered around me. It
is all the harder, because I have been successful
in the errand that brought me out here. ' I have
struck it rich,' as they say out here, and have been
able to lay by ten thousand dollars. I intended to
go home next month, carrying this with me. It
would have enabled me to start in some business
which would have yielded us a liberal living, and
provided a comfortable home for you and the children. But all this is over—for me at least. For
you I hope the money will bring what I anticipated.
I wish I could live long enough to see it in your
hands, but that cannot be.

" I have intrusted it to a friend who has been connected with me here, Thomas Butler, of Chicago.
He has solemnly promised to seek you out, and put
the money into your hands. I think he will be true
to his trust. Indeed I have no doubt on the subject,
for I cannot conceive of any man being base enough
to belie the confidence placed in him by a dying
man, and despoil a widow and her fatherless children. No, I will not permit myself to doubt the
integrity of my friend. If I should, it would make
my last sickness exceedingly bitter.

" Yet, as something might happen to Butler on
his way home, though exceedingly improbable, I
think it well to describe him to you. He is a man of
nearly fifty, I should say, about five feet ten inches
in height, with a dark complexion, and dark hair a

little tinged with gray. He will weigh about one hundred and sixty pounds. But there is one striking mark about him which will serve to identify him. He has a wart on the upper part of his right cheek—a mark which disfigures him and mortifies him exceedingly. He has consulted a physician about its removal, but has been told that the operation would involve danger, and, moreover, would not be effectual, as the wart is believed to be of a cancerous nature, and would in all probability grow out again. For these reasons he has given up his intention of having it removed, and made up his mind, unwillingly enough, to carry it to the grave with him.

"I have given you this long description, not because it seemed at all necessary, for I believe Thomas Butler to be a man of strict honesty, but because for some reason I am impelled to do so.

"I am very tired, and I feel that I must close. God bless you, dear wife, and guard our children, soon to be fatherless!

"Your loving husband,

"FREDERICK WALTON."

"P. S.—Butler has left for the East. This letter I have given to another friend to mail after my death."

CHAPTER III

LUKE FORMS A RESOLUTION

As Luke read this letter his pleasant face became stern in its expression. They had indeed been cruelly wronged. The large sum of which they had been defrauded would have insured them comfort and saved them from many an anxiety. His mother would not have been obliged to take in sewing, and he himself could have carried out his cherished design of obtaining a college education.

This man in whom his father had reposed the utmost confidence had been false to his trust. He had kept in his own hands the money which should have gone to the widow and children of his dying friend. Could anything be more base?

"Mother," said Luke, "this man Thomas Butler must be a villain."

"Yes, Luke; he has done us a great wrong."

"He thought, no doubt, that we should never hear of this money."

"I almost wish I had not, Luke. It is very tantalizing to think how it would have improved our condition."

"Then you are sorry to receive the letter, mother?"

"No, Luke. It seems like a message from the dead, and shows me how good and thoughtful your poor father was to the last. He meant to leave us comfortable."

"But his plans were defeated by a rascal. Mother, I should like to meet and punish this Thomas Butler."

"Even if you should meet him, Luke, you must be prudent. He is probably a rich man."

"Made so at our expense," added Luke, bitterly.

"And he would deny having received anything from your father."

"Mother," said Luke, sternly and deliberately, "I feel sure that I shall some day meet this man face to face, and if I do it will go hard if I don't force him to give up this money which he has falsely converted to his own use."

The boy spoke with calm and resolute dignity, hardly to be expected in one so young, and with a deep conviction that surprised his mother.

"Luke," she said, "I hardly know you to-night. You don't seem like a boy. You speak like a man."

"I feel so, mother. It is the thought of this man, triumphant in his crime, that makes me feel older than I am. Now, mother, I feel that I have a purpose in life. It is to find this man, and punish him for what he has done, unless he will make reparation."

Mrs. Walton shook her head. It was not from her that Luke had inherited his independent spirit.

She was a fond mother, of great amiability, but of a timid, shrinking disposition, which led her to deprecate any aggressive steps.

"Promise me not to get yourself into any trouble, Luke," she said, "even if you do meet this man."

"I can't promise that, mother, for I may not be able to help it. Besides, I haven't met him yet, and, as President Lincoln says, it isn't necessary to cross a bridge till you get to it. Now let us talk of something else."

"How much did you make to-day, Luke?" asked Bennie, his young brother, seven years old.

"I didn't make my fortune, Bennie. Including the morning papers, I only made sixty cents."

"That seems a good deal to me, Luke," said his mother. "I only made twenty-five. They pay such small prices for making shirts."

"I should think they did. And yet you worked harder and more steadily than I did, I have no doubt."

"I have worked since morning, probably about eight hours."

"Then you have made only three cents an hour. What a shame!"

"If I had a sewing machine, I could do more, but that is beyond our means."

"I hope soon to be able to get you one, mother. I can pay something down and the rest on installments."

"That would be quite a relief, Luke."

"If you had a sewing machine, perhaps I could help you," suggested Bennie.

"I should hardly dare to let you try, Bennie. Suppose you spoiled a shirt. It would take off two days' earnings. But I'll tell you what you can do. You can set the table, and wash the dishes, and relieve me in that way."

"Or you might take in washing," said Luke, with a laugh. "That pays better than sewing. Just imagine how nice it would look in an advertisement in the daily papers: 'A boy of seven is prepared to wash and iron for responsible parties. Address Bennie Walton, No. 161½ Green Street, near Milwaukee Avenue.'"

"Now you are laughing at me, Luke," said Bennie, pouting. "Why don't you let me go out with you and sell papers? I have seen newsboys no bigger than I am."

"I hope, Bennie," said Luke, gravely, "you will never have to go into the street with papers. I know what it is, and how poor boys fare. One night last week, at the corner of Monroe and Clark Streets, I saw a poor little chap, no older than you, selling papers at eleven o'clock. He had a dozen papers which he was likely to have left on his hands, for there are not many who will buy papers at that hour."

"Did you speak to him, Luke?" asked Benny, interested.

"Yes; I told him he ought to go home. But he

said that if he went home with all those papers unsold, his stepfather would whip him. There were tears in the poor boy's eyes as he spoke."

" What did you do, Luke? "

" I'll tell you what I did, Bennie. I thought of you, and I paid him the cost price on his papers. It wasn't much, for they were all penny papers, but the poor little fellow seemed so relieved."

" Did you sell them yourself, Luke? "

" I sold four of them. I went over to Madison Street, and stood in front of McVicker's Theater just as the people were coming out. It so happened that four persons bought papers, so I was only two cents out, after all. You remember, mother, that was the evening I got home so late."

" Yes, Luke, I felt worried about you. But you did right. I am always glad to have you help those who are worse off than we are. How terribly I should feel if Bennie had to be out late in the streets like that! "

" There are many newsboys as young, or at any rate not much older. I have sometimes seen gentlemen, handsomely dressed, and evidently with plenty of money, speak roughly to these young boys. It always makes me indignant. Why should they have so easy a time, while there are so many who don't know where their next meal is coming from? Why, what such a man spends for his meals in a single day would support a poor newsboy in comfort for a week."

"My dear Luke, this is a problem that has puzzled older and wiser heads than yours. There must always be poor people, but those who are more fortunate ought at least to give them sympathy. It is the least acknowledgment they can make for their own more favored lot."

"I am going out a little while this evening, mother."

"Very well, Luke. Don't be late."

"No, mother, I won't. I want to call on a friend of mine who is sick."

"Who is it, Luke?"

"It is Jim Norman. The poor boy took cold one day, his shoes were so far gone. He has a bad cough, and I am afraid it will go very hard with him."

"Is he a newsboy, too, Luke?" asked Bennie Walton.

"No; he is a bootblack."

"I shouldn't like to black boots."

"Nor I, Bennie; but if a boy is lucky there is more money to be made in that business."

"Where does he live?" asked Mrs. Walton.

"On Ohio Street, not very far from here. There's another boy I know lives on that street—Tom Brooks; but he isn't a friend of mine. He wanted me to keep the five dollars, and treat him and some other boys to an evening at the theater, and a supper afterwards."

"I hope you won't associate with him, Luke"

"Not more than I can help."

Luke took his hat and went downstairs into the street.

In the hall he met Nancy. She waylaid him with an eager look on her face.

"Who was the letter from, Luke?" she asked.

"From a friend of the family, who is now dead," answered Luke, gravely.

"Good gracious! How could he write it after he was dead?" ejaculated Nancy. "And how did it come to smell so of tobacco?"

"It was given to a person to mail who forgot all about it, and carried it in his pocket for a year."

"My sakes alive! If I got a letter from a dead man it would make me creep all over. No wonder your ma came near faintin'."

CHAPTER IV

AN ATTACK IN THE DARK

Luke turned into Milwaukee Avenue, and a few steps took him to West Ohio Street, where his friend lived. On the way he met Tom Brooks, who was lounging in front of a cigar store, smoking a cigarette.

"Good-evening, Tom," said Luke, politely.

"Evenin'!" responded Tom, briefly. "Where you goin'?"

"To see Jim Norman. He's sick."

"What's the matter of him?"

"He's got a bad cold, and is confined to the house."

Tom shrugged his shoulders.

"I don't go much on Jim Norman," he said. "He ought to be a girl. He never smoked a cigarette in his life."

"Didn't he? All the better for him. I don't smoke myself."

"You have smoked."

"Yes, I used to, but it troubled my mother, and I promised her I wouldn't do it again."

"So you broke off?"

20

" Yes."

" I wouldn't be tied to a woman's apron strings," said Tom, in a derisive tone.

" Wouldn't you try to oblige your mother? "

" No, I wouldn't. What does a woman know about boys? If I was a gal it would be different."

" Then we don't agree, that is all."

" I say, Luke, won't you take me to the theayter? "

" I can't afford it."

" That's all bosh! Haven't you got five dollars? I'd feel rich on five dollars."

" Perhaps I might if it were mine, but it isn't."

" You can use it all the same," said Tom, in an insinuating voice.

" Yes, I can be dishonest if I choose, but I don't choose."

" What Sunday school do you go to? " asked Tom, with a sneer.

" None at present."

" I thought you did by your talk. It makes me sick! "

" Then," said Luke, good-naturedly, " there is no need to listen to it. I am afraid you are not likely to enjoy my company, so I will walk along."

Luke kept on his way, leaving Tom smoking sullenly.

" That feller's a fool! " he muttered, in a disgusted tone.

" What feller? "

Tom turned, and saw his friend and chum, Pat O'Connor, who had just come up.

" What feller? Why, Luke Walton, of course "

" What's the matter of him? "

" He's got five dollars, and he won't pay me into the theayter."

" Where did he get such a pile of money? " asked Pat, in surprise.

" A gentleman gave it to him for a paper, tellin' him to bring the change to-morrer."

" Is he goin' to do it? "

" Yes; that's why I call him a fool."

" I wish you and I had his chance," said Pat, enviously. " We'd paint the town red, I guess."

Tom nodded. He and Pat were quite agreed on that point.

" Where's Luke goin'? " asked Pat.

" To see Jim Norman. Jim's sick with a cold."

" What time's he comin' home? "

" I don't know. Why? "

" Do you think he's got the money with him—the five-dollar bill? "

" What are you up to? " asked Tom, with a quick glance at his companion.

" I was thinkin' we might borrer the money," answered Pat, with a grin.

To Tom this was a new suggestion, but it was favorably received. He conferred with Pat in a low tone, and then the two sauntered down the street in the direction of Jim Norman's home.

Meanwhile we will follow Luke.

He kept on till he reached a shabby brick house, which had once seen better days, but so far back that there was no trace of them left.

Jim and his mother, with two smaller children, occupied two small rooms on the top floor. Luke had been there before, and did not stop to inquire directions, but ascended the stairs till he came to Jim's room. The door was partly open, and he walked in.

"How's Jim, Mrs. Norman?" he asked.

Mrs. Norman, a worn and weary woman, was washing dishes at the sink.

"He's right sick, Luke," she answered, turning round, and recognizing the visitor. "Do you hear him cough?"

From a small inner room came the sound of a hard and rasping cough.

"How are you feeling, Jim?" inquired Luke, entering, and taking a chair at the bedside.

"I don't feel any better, Luke," answered the sick boy, his face lighting up with pleasure as he recognized his friend. "I'm glad you come."

"You've got a hard cough."

"Yes; it hurts my throat when I cough, and I can't get a wink of sleep."

"I've brought you a little cough medicine. It was some we had in the house."

"Thank you, Luke. You're a good friend to me. Give me some, please."

" If your mother'll give me a spoon, I'll pour some out."

When the medicine was taken, the boys began to talk.

" I ought to be at work," said Jim, sighing. " I don't know how we'll get along if I don't get out soon. Mother has some washing to do, but it isn't enough to pay all our expenses. I used to bring in seventy-five cents a day, and that, with what mother could earn, kept us along."

" I wish I was rich enough to help you, Jim, but you know how it is. All I can earn I have to carry home. My mother sews for a house on State Street, but sewing doesn't pay as well as washing."

" I know you'd help me if you could, Luke. You have helped me by bringing in the medicine, and it does me good to have you call."

" But I would like to do more. I'll tell you what I will do. I know a rich gentleman, one of my customers. I am to call upon him to-morrow. I'll tell him about you, and perhaps he will help you."

" Any help would be acceptable, Luke, if you don't mind asking him."

" I wouldn't like to ask for myself, but I don't mind asking for you."

Luke stayed an hour, and left Jim much brighter and more cheerful for his visit.

When he went out into the street it was quite dark, although the moon now and then peeped out from behind the clouds that a brisk breeze sent

scurrying across the sky. Having a slight headache, he thought he would walk it off, so he sauntered slowly in the direction of the business portion
of the city.

Walking farther than he intended, he found himself, almost before he was aware, crossing one of the
numerous bridges that span the river. He was
busy with thoughts of Jim, and how he could help
him, and did not notice that two boys were following him stealthily. It was a complete surprise to
him therefore when they rushed upon him, and,
each seizing an arm, rendering him helpless.

Luke was not long left in doubt as to their inten-
tions.

" Hand over what money you've got, and be quick
about it! " demanded one of the boys in a hoarse
whisper.

CHAPTER V

HOW LUKE ESCAPED

The attack was so sudden and unexpected that Luke was for the moment incapable of resistance, though in general quite ready to defend himself. It was not till he felt a hand in his pocket that he "pulled himself together," as the English express it, and began to make things lively for his assailants.

"What are you after?" he demanded. "Do you want to rob me?"

"Give us the money, and be quick about it."

"How do you know I have any money?" asked Luke, beginning to suspect in whose hands he was.

"Never mind how! Hand over that five-dollar bill," was the reply, in the same hoarse whisper.

"I know you now. You're Tom Brooks," said Luke. "You're in bad business."

"No, I'm not Tom Brooks." It was Pat who spoke now. "Come, we have no time to lose. Stephen, give me your knife."

The name was a happy invention of Pat's to throw Luke off the scent. He was not himself acquainted with our hero, and did not fear identification.

26

"One of you two is Tom Brooks," said Luke, firmly. "You'd better give up this attempt at highway robbery. If I summon an officer you're liable to a long term of imprisonment. I'll save you trouble by telling you that I haven't any money with me, except a few pennies."

"Where's the five-dollar bill?"

It was Tom who spoke now.

"I left it at home with my mother. It's lucky I did, though you would have found it hard to get it from me."

"I don't believe it," said Tom, in a tone betraying disappointment.

"You may search me if you like; but if a policeman comes by you'd better take to your heels."

The boys appeared disconcerted.

"Is he lying?" asked Pat.

"No," responded Tom. "He'd own up if he had the money."

"Thank you for believing me. It is very evident that one of you knows me. Good-night. You'd better find some other way of getting money."

"Wait a minute! Are you going to tell on us? It wouldn't be fair to Tom Brooks. He ain't here, but you might get him into trouble."

"I shan't get you into trouble, Tom, but I'm afraid you bring trouble on yourself."

Apparently satisfied with this promise, the two boys slunk away in the darkness, and Luke was left to proceed on his way unmolested.

"I wouldn't have believed that of Tom," thought Luke. "I'm sorry it happened. If it had been anyone but me, and a cop had come by, it would have gone hard with him. It's lucky I left the money with mother, though I don't think they'd have got it at any rate."

Luke did not acquaint his mother with the attempt that had been made to rob him. He well knew that it would have made her very anxious for him whenever he left the house. He merely told of his visit and of the sad plight of the little bootblack.

"I would like to have helped him, mother," Luke concluded. "If we hadn't been robbed of that money father sent us——"

"We could afford the luxury of doing good," said his mother, finishing the sentence for him.

Luke's face darkened with justifiable anger.

"I know it is wrong to hate anyone, mother," he said; "but I am afraid I hate that man Thomas Butler whom I have never seen."

"It is sometimes hard to feel like a Christian, Luke," said his mother.

"This man must be one of the meanest of men. No doubt he is living in luxury while we are living from hand to mouth. Suppose you or I should fall sick! What would become of us?"

"We won't borrow trouble, Luke. Let us rather thank God for our present good health. If I should be sick it would not be as serious as if you were to become so, for you earn more than twice as much as I do."

"It ought not to be so, mother, for you work harder than I do."

"When I get a sewing machine I shall be able to contribute more to the common fund."

"I hope that will be soon. Has Bennie gone to bed?"

"Yes, he is fast asleep."

"I hope fortune will smile on us before he is much older than I. I can't bear the idea of sending him into the street among bad boys."

"I have been accustomed to judge of the news-boys by my son. Are there many bad boys among them?"

"Many of them are honest, hard-working boys, but there are some black sheep among them. I know one boy who tried to commit highway robbery, stopping a person whom he had seen with money."

"Did he get caught?"

"No, he failed of his purpose, and no complaint was made of him, though his intended victim knew who his assailant was."

"I am glad of that. It would have been hard for his poor mother if he had been convicted and sent to prison."

This Mrs. Walton said without a suspicion that it was Luke that the boy had tried to rob. When Luke heard his mother's comment he was glad that he had agreed to overlook Tom's fault.

The next morning Luke went as usual to the vicinity of the Sherman House, and began to sell papers. He looked in vain for Tom Brooks, who did not show up.

"Where is Tom Brooks?" he asked of one of Tom's friends.

"Tom's goin' to try another place," said the boy. "He says there's too many newsboys round this corner. He thinks he can do better somewheres else."

"Where is he? Do you know?"

"I seed him near the corner of Dearborn, in front of the 'Saratoga.'"

"The Saratoga" is a well-known restaurant on Dearborn Street, which is the financial street of Chicago, and given up largely to bankers, brokers, and trust companies.

"Well, I hope he'll make out well," said Luke.

Luke had the five-dollar bill in his pocket, but he knew that it was too early for the offices on La Salle Street to be open. He decided to wait till about ten o'clock, when he might be reasonably sure to find Mr. Afton.

Luke's stock of morning papers included the Chicago *Tribune*, the *Times, Herald,* and *Inter-Ocean.* He seldom disposed of his entire stock as early as ten o'clock, but this morning another newsboy in addition to Tom was absent, and Luke experienced the advantage of diminished competition. As he sold the last paper the clock struck ten.

"I think it will do for me to go to Mr. Afton's office now," thought Luke. "If I don't find him in I will wait."

La Salle Street runs parallel with Clark. It is a busy thoroughfare, and contains many buildings cut up into offices. This was the case with No. 155.

Luke entered the building and scanned the directory on either side of the door. He had no difficulty in finding the name of Benjamin Afton.

He had to go up two flights of stairs, for Mr. Afton's office was on the third floor.

CHAPTER VI

MR. AFTON'S OFFICE

Mr. Afton's office was of unusual size, and fronted on La Salle Street. As Luke entered he observed that it was furnished better than the ordinary business office. Indeed, it seemed to the occupant the part of wisdom to make the room where he spent so many hours of his time as comfortable and even as luxurious as his means would justify. On the floor was a handsome Turkey carpet. The desks were of some rich dark wood, and the chairs were as costly as those in his library. In a closed bookcase at one end of the room, surmounted by bronze statuettes, was a full library of reference.

At one desk stood a tall man, perhaps thirty-five, with red hair and prominent features. At another desk was a young fellow of eighteen, bearing a marked resemblance to the head bookkeeper. There was besides a young man of perhaps twenty-two, sitting at a table, apparently filing bills.

" Mr. Afton must be a rich man to have such an elegant office," thought Luke.

The red-haired bookkeeper did not take the trouble to look up to see who had entered the office.

"Is Mr. Afton in?" Luke asked, in a respectful tone.

The bookkeeper raised his eyes for a moment, glanced at Luke with a supercilious air, and said curtly, "No!"

"Do you know when he will be in?" continued the newsboy.

"Quite indefinite. What is your business, boy?"

"My business is with Mr. Afton," Luke answered.

"Humph! is it of an important nature?" asked the bookkeeper with a sneer, as he remarked the plain, well-worn suit of the young visitor.

Luke smiled.

"It is not very important," he answered, "but I wish to see Mr. Afton personally."

"Whose office are you in?"

"He isn't in any office, Uncle Nathaniel," put in the red-haired boy. "He is a common newsboy. I see him every morning round the Sherman House."

"Ha! is that so? Boy, we don't want to buy any papers, nor does Mr. Afton, I am sure. You can go."

As the bookkeeper spoke he pointed to the door.

"I have no papers to sell," said Luke, rather provoked; "but I come here on business with Mr. Afton, and will take the liberty to wait till he comes."

"Oh, my eyes! Ain't he got cheek?" ejaculated

the red-haired boy. "I say, boy, do you black
boots as well as sell papers?"

"No, I don't."

"Some of the newsboys do. I thought, perhaps,
you had got a job to black Mr. Afton's boots
every morning."

Luke, who was a spirited boy, was fast getting
angry.

"I don't want to interfere with you in any way,"
he said.

"What do you mean?" demanded the red-haired
boy, his cheeks rivaling his hair in color.

"I thought that might be one of your duties."

"Why, you impudent young vagabond! Uncle
Nathaniel, did you hear that?"

"Boy, you had better go," said the bookkeeper,
waving his hand.

"You can leave your card," added Eustis Clark,
the nephew.

Now it so happened that a friend of Luke's had
printed and given him a dozen cards a few days
previous, and he had them in his pocket at that
moment.

"Thank you for the suggestion," he said, and
walking up to the boy's desk he deposited on it a
card bearing this name in neat script:

LUKE WALTON.

"Be kind enough to hand that to Mr. Afton," he
said.

Eustis held up the card, and burst into a guffaw. "Well, I never!" he ejaculated. "No, I never did. Mr. Walton, your most obedient," he concluded, with a ceremonious bow.

"The same to you!" said Luke, with a smile.

"I never saw a newsboy put on such airs before," he said, as Luke left the office. "Did you, Uncle Nathaniel? Do you think he really had any business with the boss?"

"Probably he wanted to supply the office with papers. Now stop fooling, and go to work."

"They didn't seem very glad to see me," thought Luke. "I want to see Mr. Afton this morning, or he may think that I have not kept my word about the money."

Luke stationed himself in the doorway at the entrance to the building, meaning to intercept Mr. Afton as he entered from the street. He had to wait less than ten minutes. Mr. Afton smiled in instant recognition as he saw Luke, and seemed glad to see him.

"I am glad the boy justified my idea of him," he said to himself. "I would have staked a thousand dollars on his honesty. Such a face as that doesn't belong to a rogue."

"I am rather late," he said. "Have you been here long?"

"Not very long, sir; I have been up in your office."

"Why didn't you sit down and wait for me?"

"I don't think the red-haired gentleman cared
to have me. The boy asked me to leave my
card."

Mr. Afton looked amused.

"And did you?" he asked.

"Yes, sir."

"Do you generally carry visiting cards?" asked
Mr. Afton, in some surprise.

"Well, I happened to have some with me this
morning."

"Please show me one. So your name is Luke
Walton?" he added, glancing at the card.

"Yes, sir; office corner Clark and Randolph
Streets."

"I will keep the card and bear it in mind."

"I have brought your change, sir," said Luke,
putting his hand in his pocket.

"You can come upstairs and pay it to me in the
office. It will be more business-like."

Luke was glad to accept the invitation, for it
would prove to the skeptical office clerks that he
really had business with their employer.

Eustis Clark and his uncle could not conceal their
surprise when they saw Luke follow Mr. Afton
into the office.

There was a smaller room inclosed at one corner,
which was especially reserved for Mr. Afton.

"Come here, Luke," said he, pleasantly.

Luke followed him inside.

He drew from his pocket four dollars and ninety-

eight cents, and laid it on the table behind which
his patron had taken a seat.

"Won't you please count it and see if it is
right?" he asked.

"I can see that it is, Luke. I am afraid I have
put you to more trouble than the profit on the two
papers I bought would pay for."

"Not at all, sir. Besides, it's all in the way of
business. I thank you for putting confidence in
me."

"I thought I was not mistaken in you, and the
result shows that I was right. My boy, I saw that
you had an honest face. I am sure that the thought
of keeping back the money never entered your .
head."

"No, sir, it did not, though one of the newsboys
advised me to keep it."

"It would have been very short-sighted as a matter of policy. I will take this money, but I want to
encourage you in the way of well-doing."

He drew from his vest pocket a bill, and extended it to Luke.

"It isn't meant as a reward for honesty, but
only as a mark of the interest I have begun to feel
in you."

"Thank you, sir," said Luke; and as he took the
bill, he started in surprise, for it was ten dollars.

"Did you mean to give as much as this?" he
asked doubtfully.

"How much is it?"

" Ten dollars."

" I thought it was five, but I am glad it is more. Yes, Luke, you are welcome to it. Have you anyone dependent upon you?"

" My mother. She will be very much pleased."

" That's right, my lad. Always look out for your mother. You owe her a debt which you can never repay."

" That is true, sir. But I would like to use a part of this money for someone else."

" For yourself?"

" No; for a friend."

Then he told in simple language of Jim Norman, and how seriously his family was affected by his sickness and enforced illness.

" Jim has no money to buy medicine," he concluded. " If you don't object, Mr. Afton, I will give Jim's mother half this money, after buying some cough medicine out of it."

The merchant listened with approval.

" I am glad, Luke, you feel for others," he said, " but I can better afford to help your friend than you. Here is a five-dollar bill. Tell the boy it is from a friend, and if he should need more let me know."

" Thank you, sir," said Luke, fairly radiant as he thought of Jim's delight. " I won't take up any more of your time, but will bid you good-morning."

Probably Mr. Afton wished to give his clerks a lesson, for he followed Luke to the door of the

outer office, and shook hands cordially with him,
saying: " I shall be glad to have you call, when you
wish to see me, Luke; " adding, " I may possibly
have some occasional work for you to do. If so, I
know where to find you."

" Thank you, sir."

" What's got into the old man? " thought Eustis
Clark. " He treats that young ragamuffin as
if he were the president of the bank. No wonder
the boy puts on airs and carries visiting cards."

As Mr. Afton returned to his sanctum, Eustis
said with a grin, holding up the card:

" Mr. Walton left his card for you, thinking you
might not be in time to see him."

" Give it to me, if you please," and the rich man
took the card without a smile, and put it into his
vest pocket, not seeming in the least surprised.

" Mr. Walton called to pay me some money," he
said, gravely. " Whenever he calls invite him to
wait till my return."

" Well, I never did! " ejaculated Eustis, rubbing
an imaginary mustache in his perplexity. " To
treat a common newsboy that way! I wonder if
the old man's losing his intellect."

CHAPTER VII

A STRANGE ENCOUNTER

Luke went home that evening in high spirits. The gift he had received from Mr. Afton enabled him to carry out a plan he had long desired to realize, but had been prevented from so doing by poverty. It was to secure a sewing machine for his mother, and thus increase her earnings while diminishing her labors. He stopped at an establishment not far from Clark Street, and entering the showroom, asked: " What is the price of your sewing machines? "

" One in a plain case will cost you twenty-five dollars."

" Please show me one."

" Do you want it for your wife?" asked the salesman, smiling.

" She may use it some time. My mother will use it first."

The salesman pointed out an instrument with which Luke was well pleased.

" Would you like to see how it works? "

" Yes, please."

" Miss Morris, please show this young man how to operate the machine."

In the course of ten minutes Luke got a fair idea of the method of operating.

"Do you require the whole amount down?" asked Luke.

"No; we sell on installments, if preferred."

"What are your terms?"

"Five dollars first payment, and then a dollar a week, with interest on the balance till paid. Of course a customer is at liberty to shorten the time of payment if he prefers."

"Then I think I will engage one," Luke decided.

"Very well! Come up to the desk, and give me your name and address. On payment of five dollars, we will give you a receipt on account, specifying the terms of paying the balance, etc."

Luke transacted his business, and made arrangements to have the machine delivered any time after six o'clock, when he knew he would be at home.

"That's a good job," he said to himself. "And the best of it is, I've got five dollars left, to fall back upon in case of bad luck. It will pay five weeks' installments, if I don't succeed in saving enough in any other way."

As Luke was coming out of the sewing-machine office he saw Tom Brooks just passing. Tom looked a little uneasy, not feeling certain whether Luke had recognized him as one of his assailants or not the evening previous.

Luke felt that he had a right to be angry. Indeed, he had it in his power to have Tom arrested,

and charged with a very serious crime—that o‡
highway robbery. But his good luck made him
good-natured.

"Good-evening, Tom," he said. "I didn't see
you selling papers to-day."

"No; I was on Dearborn Street.

"He doesn't know it was me," thought Tom,
congratulating himself, and added: "Have you
been buying a sewing machine?"

This was said in joke.

"Yes," answered Luke, considerably to Tom's
surprise. "I have bought one."

"How much?"

"Twenty-five dollars."

"Where did you raise twenty-five dollars?
You're foolin'."

"I bought it on the installment plan. I paid five
dollars down."

"Oho!" said Tom, nodding significantly. "I
know where you got that money?"

"Where did I?"

"From the gentleman that bought a couple of
papers yesterday."

"You hit it right the first time."

"I thought you weren't no better than the rest of
us—you that pretended to be so extra honest."

"What do you mean by that, Tom Brooks?"

"You pretended that you were going to give back
the man's change, and spent it, after all. I thought
you weren't such a saint as you pretended to be."

"I see you keep on judging me by yourself, Tom Brooks. I took round the money this morning, and he gave it to me."

"Is that true?"

"Yes; I generally tell the truth."

"Then you're lucky. If I'd returned it, he wouldn't have given me a cent."

"It's best to be honest on all occasions," said Luke, looking significantly at Tom, who colored up, for he now saw that he had been recognized the night before.

Tom sneaked off on some pretext, and Luke kept on his way home.

"Did you do well to-day, Luke?" asked Bennie.

"Yes, Bennie; very well."

"How much did you make?"

"I'll tell you by and by. Mother, can I help you about the supper?"

"You may toast the bread, Luke. I am going to have your favorite dish—milk toast."

"All right, mother. Have you been sewing to-day?"

"Yes, Luke. I sat so long in one position that I got cramped."

"I wish you had a sewing machine."

"So do I, Luke; but I must be patient. A sewing machine costs more money than we can afford."

"One can be got for twenty-five dollars, I have heard."

" That is a good deal of money to people in our position."

" We may as well hope for one. I shouldn't be surprised if we were able to buy a sewing machine very soon."

Meanwhile Luke finished toasting the bread, and his mother was dipping it in milk when a rapid step was heard on the stairway, the door was unceremoniously opened, and Nancy's red head was thrust into the room.

" Please, Mrs. Walton," said Nancy, breathlessly, " there's a man downstairs with a sewing machine which he says is for you."

" There must be some mistake, Nancy. I haven't ordered any sewing machine."

" Shall I send him off, ma'am? "

" No, Nancy," said Luke; " it's all right. I'll go downstairs and help him bring it up."

" How is this, Luke? " asked Mrs. Walton, bewildered.

" I'll explain afterwards, mother."

Up the stairs and into the room came the sewing machine, and was set down near the window. Bennie surveyed it with wonder and admiration.

When the man who brought it was gone, Luke explained to his mother how it had all come about.

" You see, mother, you didn't have to wait long," he concluded.

" I feel deeply thankful, Luke," said Mrs. Walton. " I can do three times the work I have been accustomed to do, and in much less time. This Mr. Afton must be a kind and charitable man."

"I like him better than his clerks," said Luke. "There is a red-headed bookkeeper and a boy there who tried to snub me, and keep me out of the office. I try to think well of red-headed people on account of Nancy, but I can't say I admire them."

After supper Luke gave his mother a lesson in operating the machine. Both found that it required a little practice, but Mrs. Walton felt sure that in a day or two she would become familiar with its use.

The next morning as Luke was standing at his usual corner, he had a surprise.

A gentleman came out of the Sherman House and walked slowly up Clark Street. As he passed Luke, he stopped and asked, "Boy, have you the *Inter-Ocean?*"

Luke naturally looked up in his customer's face while he was picking out the paper. He paused in the greatest excitement.

The man was on the shady side of fifty, nearly six feet in height, with a dark complexion, hair tinged with gray, and a wart on the upper part of his right cheek!

CHAPTER VIII

A MARKED MAN

At last, so Luke verily believed, he stood face to face with the man who had deceived his dying father, and defrauded his mother and himself of a sum which would wholly change their positions and prospects. But he wanted to know positively, and he could not think of a way to acquire this knowledge.

Meanwhile the gentleman noticed the boy's scrutiny, and it did not please him.

"Well, boy!" he said gruffly, "you seem determined to know me again. You stare hard enough. Let me tell you this is not good manners."

"Excuse me," said Luke, "but your face looked familiar to me. I thought I had seen you before."

"Very likely you have. I come to Chicago frequently, and generally stop at the Sherman House."

"Probably that explains it," said Luke. "Are you not Mr. Thomas, of St. Louis?"

The gentleman laughed.

"You will have to try again," he said. "I am Mr. Browning, of Milwaukee. Thomas is my first nar— "

"Browning!" thought Luke, disappointed. "Evidently I am on the wrong track. And yet he answers father's description exactly."

"I don't know anyone in Milwaukee," he said aloud.

"Then it appears we can't claim acquaintance."

The gentleman took his paper and turned down Randolph Street toward State.

"Strange!" he soliloquized, "that boy's interest in my personal appearance. I wonder if there can be a St. Louis man who resembles me. If so, he can't be a very good-looking man. This miserable wart ought to be enough to distinguish me from anyone else."

He paused a minute, and then a new thought came into his mind.

"There is something familiar in that boy's face. I wonder who he can be. I will buy my evening papers of him, and take that opportunity to inquire."

Meanwhile Luke, to satisfy a doubt in his mind, entered the hotel, and, going up to the office, looked over the list of arrivals. He had to turn back a couple of pages and found this entry:

"THOMAS BROWNING, Milwaukee."

"His name is Browning, and he does come from Milwaukee," he said to himself. "I thought, perhaps, he might have given me a false name, though he could have no reason for doing so."

Luke felt that he must look farther for the man who had betrayed his father's confidence.

"I didn't think there could be two men of such a peculiar appearance," he reflected. "Surely there can't be three. If I meet another who answers the description I shall be convinced that he is the man I am after."

In the afternoon the same man approached Luke, as he stood on his accustomed corner.

"You may give me the *Mail* and *Journal*," he said.

"Yes, sir; here they are. Three cents."

"I believe you are the boy who recognized me, or thought you did, this morning."

"Yes, sir."

"If you ever run across this Mr. Thomas, of St. Louis, present him my compliments, will you?"

"Yes, sir," answered Luke, with a smile.

"By the way, what is your name?"

"Luke Walton."

The gentleman started.

"Luke Walton!" he repeated, slowly, eying the newsboy with a still closer scrutiny.

"Yes, sir."

"It's a new name to me. Can't your father find a better business for you than selling papers?"

"My father is dead, sir."

"Dead!" repeated Browning, slowly. "That is unfortunate for you. How long has he been dead?"

"About two years."

"What did he die of?"

"I don't know, sir, exactly. He died away from home—in California."

There was a strange look, difficult to read, on the gentleman's face.

"That is a long way off," he said. "I have always thought I should like to visit California. I have often promised myself that pleasure. When my business will permit I will take a trip out that way."

Here was another difference between Mr. Browning and the man of whom Luke's father had written. The stranger had never been in California.

Browning handed Luke a silver quarter in payment for the papers.

"Never mind about the change," he said, with a wave of his hand.

"Thank you, sir. You are very kind."

If Luke could have divined the thoughts of the man who had treated him thus generously, he would have felt less grateful.

"This must be the son of my old California friend," Browning said to himself. "Can he have heard of the money intrusted to me? I don't think it possible, for I left Walton on the verge of death. That money has made my fortune. I invested it in land which has more than quadrupled in value. Old women say that honesty pays," he added, with a sneer; "but it is nonsense. In this case dishonesty has paid me richly. If the boy has heard any-thing, it is lucky that I changed my name to Brown-ing out of deference to my wife's aunt, in return for a beggarly three thousand dollars. However, I have made it up to ten thousand dollars by judicious investment. My young newsboy acquaint-ance will find it hard to identify me with the Thomas Butler who took charge of his father's money."

If Browning had been possessed of a conscience it might have troubled him when he was brought face to face with one of the sufferers from his crime; but he was a hard, selfish man, to whom his own interests were of supreme importance. There are many such men, unfortunately, who, with-out compunction, build up their fortunes on the sufferings and losses of widows and orphans.

Even to Thomas Browning there came the thought, " If I could give the boy fifty dollars with-out arousing suspicion I would do so. But, after all, he is getting on well enough. I have heard that these newsboys make a good deal of money. I had better let well enough alone. As long as they don't know of the money, they won't regret its loss."

In this way Browning quieted the slight protest of his almost callous conscience, and no longer allowed himself to be annoyed by the thought of the family he had cruelly wronged.

" He'll never know it, and I needn't allow it to disturb me," was his final conclusion.

But something happened within an hour which gave him a feeling of anxiety.

He was just coming out of the Chicago post office, at the corner of Adams and Clark Streets, when a hand was laid upon his shoulder.

"How are you, Butler?" said a tall man, wearing a Mexican sombrero. "I haven't set eyes upon you since we were together at Gold Gulch, in California."

Browning looked about him apprehensively, Fortunately he was some distance from the corner where Luke Walton was selling papers.

"I am well, thank you," he said.

"Are you living in Chicago?"

"No; I live in Wisconsin."

"Have you seen anything of the man you used to be with so much—Walton?"

"No; he died."

"Did he, indeed? Well, I am sorry to hear that. He was a good fellow. Did he leave anything?"

"I am afraid not."

"I thought he struck it rich."

"So he did; but he lost all he made."

"How was that?"

"Poor investments, I fancy."

"I remember he told me one day that he had scraped together seven or eight thousand dollars."

Browning shrugged his shoulders. "I think that was a mistake," he said. "Walton liked to put his best foot foremost."

"You think, then, he misrepresented?"

"I think he would have found it hard to find the sum you mention."

"You surprise me, Butler. I always looked upon Walton as a singularly reliable man."

"So he was—in most things. But let me correct you on one point. You call me Butler?"

"Isn't that your name?"

"It was, but I had a reason—a good, substantial, pecuniary reason—for changing it. I am now Thomas Browning."

"Say you so? Well, I don't say but I would change my own if someone would pay me for doing so. Are you engaged this evening?"

"Yes, unfortunately."

"I was about to invite you to some theater."

"Another time—thanks."

"I must steer clear of that man," thought Browning. "He is one of the few who knew me in California. I won't meet him again, if I can help it."

CHAPTER IX

STEPHEN WEBB

The more Browning thought of the newsboy in whom he had so strangely recognized the son of the man whom he had so cruelly wronged, the more uneasy he felt.

" He has evidently heard of me," he soliloquized. " His father could not have been so near death as I supposed. He must have sent the boy or his mother a message about that money. If it should come to his knowledge that I am the Thomas Butler to whom his father confided ten thousand dollars which I have failed to hand over to the family, he may make it very disagreeable for me."

The fact that so many persons were able to identify him as Thomas Butler made the danger more imminent.

" I must take some steps—but what? " Browning asked himself.

He kept on walking till he found himself passing the entrance of a low poolroom. He never played pool, nor would it have suited a man of his social position to enter such a place, but that he caught sight of a young man, whose face and figure were

familiar to him, in the act of going into it. He
quickened his pace, and laid a hand on the young
man's shoulder.

The latter turned quickly, revealing a face bearing the unmistakable marks of dissipation.

"Uncle Thomas!" he exclaimed, apparently ill
at ease.

"Yes, Stephen, it is I. Where are you going?"
The young man hesitated.

"You need not answer. I see you are wedded to
your old amusements. Are you still in the place I
got for you?"

Stephen Webb looked uneasy and shamefaced.

"I have lost my place," he answered, after a
pause.

"How does it happen that you lost it?"

"I don't know. Someone must have prejudiced
my employer against me."

"It is your own habits that have prejudiced him,
I make no doubt."

This was true. One morning Stephen, whose
besetting sin was intemperance, appeared at the
office where he was employed in such a state of in-
toxication that he was summarily discharged. It
may be explained that he was a son of Mr. Browning's only sister.

"When were you discharged?" asked his uncle.

"Last week."

"And have you tried to get another situation?"
"Yes."

"What are your prospects of success?"

"There seem to be very few openings just now, Uncle Thomas."

"The greater reason why you should have kept the place I obtained for you. Were you going to play pool in this low place?"

"I was going to look on. A man must have some amusement," said Stephen, sullenly.

"Amusement is all you think of. However, it so happens that I have something that I wish you to do."

Stephen regarded his uncle in surprise.

"Are you going to open an office in Chicago?" he asked.

"No; the service is of a different nature. It is —secret and confidential. It is, I may say, something in the detective line."

"Then I'm your man," said his nephew, brightening up.

"The service is simple, so that you will probably be qualified to do what I require."

"I've read lots of detective stories," said Stephen, eagerly. "It's just the work I should like."

"Humph! I don't think much is to be learned from detective stories. You will understand, of course, that you are not to let anyone know you are acting for me."

"Certainly. You will find that I can keep a secret."

"I leave Chicago to-morrow morning, and will

give you directions before I go. Where can we
have a private conference?"

"Here is an oyster house. We shall be quiet
here."

"Very well! We will go in."

They entered a small room, with a sanded floor,
provided with a few unpainted tables. It seemed
quiet enough, for there were only two guests
present, seated at a table near the front.

Stephen and his uncle went to the back of the
room, and seated themselves at the rear table.

"We must order something," suggested Stephen.

"Get what you please," said Browning, indiffer-
ently.

"Two stews!" ordered Stephen. "We can talk
while they are getting them ready."

"Very well! Now, for my instructions. At the
corner of Clark and Randolph Streets every morning and evening you will find a newsboy selling
papers."

"A dozen, you mean."

"True, but I am going to describe this boy so
that you may know him. He is about fifteen, I
should judge, neatly dressed, and would be considered good-looking."

"Do you know his name?"

"Yes, it is Luke Walton."

"Is he the one I am to watch?"

"You are to make his acquaintance, and find out
all you can about his circumstances."

"Do you know where he lives?"

"No; that is one of the things you are to find out for me."

"What else do you want me to find out?"

"Find out how many there are in the family, also how they live; whether they have anything to live on except what this newsboy earns."

"All right, Uncle Thomas. You seem to have a great deal of interest in this boy."

"That is my business," said Browning, curtly. "If you wish to work for me, you must not show too much curiosity. Never mind what my motives are. Do you understand?"

"Certainly, Uncle Thomas. It shall be as you say. I suppose I am to be paid?"

"Yes. How much salary did you receive where you were last employed?"

"Ten dollars a week."

"You shall receive this sum for the present. It is very good pay for the small service required of you."

"All right, uncle."

The stews were ready by this time. They were brought and set before Stephen and his uncle. The latter toyed with his spoon, only taking a taste or two, but Stephen showed much more appreciation of the dish, not being accustomed, like his uncle, to dining at first-class hotels.

"How am I to let you know what I find out?" asked Stephen.

" Write me at Milwaukee. I will send you further
instructions from there."

" Very well, sir."

" Oh, by the way, you are never to mention me
to this Luke Walton. I have my reasons."

" I will do just as you say."

" How is your mother, Stephen? "

" About the same. She isn't a very cheerful party,
you know. She is always fretting."

" Has she any lodgers? "

" Yes, three, but one is a little irregular with his
rent."

" Of course, I expect that you will hand your
mother half the weekly sum I pay you. She has a
right to expect that much help from her son."

Stephen assented, but not with alacrity, and as
he had now disposed of the stew, the two rose from
their seats and went outside. A few words of final
instructions, and they parted.

" I wonder why Uncle Thomas takes such an
interest in that newsboy," thought Stephen. " I
will make it my business to find out."

CHAPTER X

STEPHEN WEBB OBTAINS SOME INFORMATION

Luke was at his post the following morning, and had disposed of half his papers when Stephen Webb strolled by. He walked past Luke, and then, as if it was an afterthought, turned back, and addressed him.

"Have you a morning *Tribune?*" he asked.

Luke produced it.

"How's business to-day?" asked Stephen in an off-hand manner.

"Pretty fair," answered Luke, for the first time taking notice of the inquirer, who did not impress him very favorably.

"I have often wondered how you newsboys make it pay," said Stephen, in a sociable tone.

"We don't make our fortunes, as a rule," answered Luke, smiling, "so I can't recommend you to go into it."

"I don't think it would suit me. I don't mind owning up that I am lazy. But, then, I am not obliged to work—for the present, at least."

Luke eyed him with curiosity. He did not look like a young man of means, and his suit was almost shabby, but he spoke as if he was able to live without work.

"I should like to be able to live without work," said the newsboy. "But even then I would find something to do. I should not be happy if I were idle."

"I am not wholly without work," said Stephen. "My uncle, who lives at a distance, occasionally sends to me to do something for him. I have to hold myself subject to his orders. In the meantime I get an income from him. How long have you been a newsboy?"

"Nearly two years."

"Do you like it? Why don't you get a place in a store or an office?"

"I should like to, if I could make enough; but boys get very small salaries."

"I was about to offer to look for a place for you. I know some men in business."

"Thank you! You are very kind, considering that we are strangers."

"Oh, well, I can judge of you by your looks. I shouldn't be afraid to recommend you."

Luke felt that it was ungracious, but it occurred to him that he could hardly say as much for his companion, whose face had a dissipated look that by no means recommended him.

"Thank you!" he replied; "but unless you can offer me as much as five dollars a week, I should feel obliged to keep on selling papers. I not only have myself to look out for, but a mother and little brother."

Stephen nodded to himself complacently. It was the very information of which he was in search.

"Then your father isn't living?" he said.

"No. He died in California."

"Uncle Thomas made his money in California," Stephen said to himself. "I wonder if he knew this newsboy's father.

"Five dollars is little enough for three persons to live upon," he went on, in a sympathetic manner.

"Mother earns something by sewing," Luke answered, unsuspiciously; "but it takes all we can make to support us."

"Then they can't have any other resources," thought Stephen. "I am getting on famously."

"Well, good-morning, Luke!" he said. "I'll see you later."

"How do you know my name?" asked Luke, in surprise.

"I'm an idiot!" thought Stephen. "I ought to have appeared ignorant of his name. I have seen you before to-day," he replied, taking a little time to think. "I heard one of the other newsboys calling you by name. I don't pretend to be a magician."

This explanation satisfied Luke. It appeared very natural.

"I have a great memory for names," proceeded Stephen. "That reminds me that I have not told you mine—I am Stephen Webb, at your service."

" I will remember it."

" Have a cigarette, Luke? " added Stephen, pro-
ducing a packet from his pocket.

" Thank you; I don't smoke."

" Don't smoke, and you a newsboy! I thought
all of you smoked."

" Most of us do, but I promised my mother I
wouldn't smoke till I was twenty-one."

" Then I'm old enough to smoke. I've smoked
ever since I was twelve years old—well, good-morning!

" That'll do for one day," thought Stephen Webb.
" I rather like this job. The duties are light and
easy, and it is to my advantage to make it last as
long as possible. I don't feel any particular interest in this boy, but I should like to know what my
esteemed uncle is up to. He pretends to be a man
of high respectability, but it always struck me that
there was something sly about him. However, he's
got money, and I must do what I can to please
him."

It was three days before Stephen Webb called
again on his new acquaintance. He did not wish
Luke to suspect anything, he said to himself.
Really, however, he found other things to take up
his attention. At the rate his money was going it
seemed very doubtful whether he would be able to
give his mother any part of his salary, as suggested
by his uncle.

" Hang it all! " he said to himself, as he noted his

rapidly diminishing hoard. "Why can't my uncle open his heart and give me more than ten dollars a week? Fifteen dollars wouldn't be any too much, and to him it would be nothing, positively nothing."

On the second evening Luke went home late. It had been a poor day for him, and his receipts were less than usual, though he had been out more hours.

When he entered the house, however, he assumed a cheerful look, for he never wished to depress his mother's spirits.

"You are late, Luke," said Mrs. Walton; "but I have kept your supper warm."

"What makes you so late, Luke?" asked Bennie.

"The papers went slow, Bennie. They will sometimes. There's no very important news just now. I suppose that explains it."

After a while Luke thought he noticed that his mother looked more serious than usual.

"What's the matter, mother?" he asked. "Have you a headache?"

"No, Luke. I am perfectly well, but I am feeling a little anxious."

"About what, mother?"

"I went around this afternoon to take half a dozen shirts that I had completed, and asked for more. They told me they had no more for me at present, that they had made an arrangement to have a good deal of their work done in the country, and they didn't know when I could have any more."

This was bad news, for Luke knew that he alone did not earn enough to support the family. However, he answered cheerfully: "Don't be anxious, mother! There are plenty of other establishments in Chicago besides the one you have been working for."

"That is true, Luke; but I don't know whether that will help me. I stopped at two places after leaving Gusset & Co.'s, and was told that their list was full."

"Well, mother, don't let us think of it to-night! It's of no use to borrow trouble. To-morrow we can try again."

Luke's cheerfulness had its effect on his mother, and the evening was passed socially. Mrs. Walton sewed for herself, and Luke amused Bennie by his stories of what he had seen during the day.

The next morning Luke went out to work at the usual time. He had all his papers sold out by half-past ten o'clock, and walked over to State Street, partly to fill up the time, and partly in search of some stray job. He was standing in front of the Bee Hive, a well-known drygoods store on State Street, when his attention was called to an old lady, who, in attempting to cross the street, had imprudently placed herself just in the track of a rapidly advancing cable car. Becoming sensible of her danger, the old lady uttered a terrified cry, but was too panic-stricken to move.

On came the car, with gong sounding out its

alarm, and a cry of horror went up from the by-standers.

Luke alone seemed to have his wits about him.

He saw that there was not a moment to lose, and, gathering up his strength, dashed to the old lady's assistance.

CHAPTER XI

A HOUSE ON PRAIRIE AVENUE

The old lady had just become conscious of her peril when Luke reached her. She was too bewildered to move, and would inevitably have been crushed by the approaching car had not Luke seized her by the arm, and fairly dragged her out of danger.

Then, as the car passed on, he took off his hat, and said, apologetically: " I hope you will excuse my roughness, madam, but I could see no other way of saving you."

" Please lead me to the sidewalk," gasped the old lady. Luke complied with her request.

" I am deeply thankful to you, my boy," she said, as soon as she found voice. " I can see that I was in great danger. I was busily thinking, or I should not have been so careless."

" I am glad that I was able to help you," responded Luke, as he prepared to leave his new acquaintance.

" Don't leave me!" said the old lady. " My nerves are so upset that I don't like being left alone."

"I am quite at your service, madam," replied Luke, politely. "Shall I put you on board the cars?"

"No, call a carriage, please."

This was easily done, for they were in front of the Palmer House, where a line of cabs may usually be found. Luke called one, and assisted the old lady inside.

"Where shall I tell the driver to take you?" he asked.

The old lady named a number on Prairie Avenue, which contains some of the finest residences in Chicago.

"Can I do anything more for you?" asked our hero.

"Yes," was the unexpected reply. "Get in yourself, if you can spare the time."

"Certainly," assented Luke.

He took his seat beside the old lady, wondering what further service she required of him.

"I hope you have receovered from your fright," he said, politely.

"Yes, I begin to feel myself again. Probably you wonder why I have asked you to accompany me?"

"Probably because you may need my services," suggested Luke.

"Not altogether. I shudder as I think of the danger from which you rescued me, but I have another object in view."

Luke waited for her to explain.

" I want to become better acquainted with you."

" Thank you, madam."

" I fully recognize that you have done me a great service. Now, if I ask you a fair question about yourself, you won't think it an old woman's curiosity ? "

" I hope I should not be so ill-bred, madam."

" Really, you are a very nice boy."

Luke blushed a little, for he was not used to compliments.

" Now, tell me where you live ? "

" On Green Street."

" Where is that ? "

" Only a stone's throw from Milwaukee Avenue."

" I don't think I was ever in that part of the city."

" It is not a nice part of the city, but we cannot afford to live in a better place."

" You say ' we.' Does that mean your father and mother ? "

" My father is dead. Our family consists of my mother, my little brother, and myself."

" And you are—excuse my saying so—poor ? "

" We are poor, but thus far we have not wanted for food or shelter."

" I suppose you are employed in some way ? "

" Yes ; I sell papers."

" Then you are a newsboy ? "

" Yes, madam."

" I have read about newsboys, but I know very

little about them. I suppose you cannot save very much."

" If I make seventy-five cents a day I consider myself quite lucky. It is more than I average."

" Surely you can't live on that—I mean the three of you? "

" Mother earns something by making shirts; at least, she has done so; but yesterday she was told that she would not have any more work at present."

" And your brother—he is too young to work, I suppose? "

" Yes, madam."

" I am afraid," said the old lady, thoughtfully, " that we who enjoy all that wealth can give us, and are spared all pecuniary anxieties, are not sufficiently grateful for the good gifts which Providence has bestowed upon us."

Luke knew that a reply was not expected, and he did not make any.

" Do you ever get low-spirited?" asked the old lady, suddenly.

" No; I am always hoping that better days will come."

" And your mother? "

" She is not so hopeful; but while she had work to do she was always cheerful. Last evening I found her out of spirits. You see, she can't tell when she will have work again."

" Just so. Tell her from me, to hope for better fortune."

"I will, madam."

While this conversation was going on, the cab was making rapid progress, and as the last words were spoken the driver reined up in front of a handsome residence.

"Is this the place, madam?" asked Luke.

The old lady looked out of the hack.

"Yes," she answered. "I had no idea we had got along so far."

Luke helped her out of the cab. She paid the man his fare, and then signed Luke to help her up the steps.

"I want you to come into the house with me," she said. "I have not got through talking with you."

A maidservant answered the bell. She looked surprised when she saw the old lady's young companion.

"Is my niece in?" asked the old lady.

"No, Mrs. Merton—Master Harold is in."

"Never mind! You may come upstairs with me, young man."

Luke followed the old lady up the broad, handsome staircase, stealing a curious glance at an elegantly furnished drawing room, the door of which opened into the hall.

His companion led the way into the front room on the second floor.

"Remain here until I have taken off my things." she said.

Luke seated himself in a luxurious armchair, wholly unlike the chairs in his humble home.

He looked about him and wondered how it would seem to live in such luxury. He had little time for thought, for in less than five minutes Mrs. Merton made her appearance.

"You have not yet told me your name," she said.

"Luke Walton."

"That's a good name—I am Mrs. Merton."

"I noticed that the servant called you so," said Luke.

"Yes; I am a widow. My married niece lives here with me. She is also a widow, with one son, Harold. I think he might be about your age. Her name is Tracy. You wonder why I give you all these particulars? I see you do. It is because I mean to keep up our acquaintance."

"Thank you, Mrs. Merton."

"My experience this morning has shown me that I am hardly fit to go about the city alone. Yet I am not willing to remain at home. It has occurred to me that I can make use of your services with advantage both to you and myself. What do you say?"

"I shall be glad of anything that will increase my income," said Luke, promptly.

"So I thought. Please call here to-morrow morning, and inquire for me. I will then tell you what I require."

"Very well, Mrs. Merton. You may depend upon me."

"And accept a week's pay in advance."

She put a sealed envelope into his hand. Luke took it, and, with a bow, left the room.

CHAPTER XII

A PLOT THAT FAILED

As the distance was considerable to the business part of the city, Luke boarded a car and rode downtown. It did not occur to him to open the envelope till he was halfway to the end of his journey.

When he did so, he was agreeably surprised. The envelope contained a ten-dollar bill.

" Ten dollars! Hasn't Mrs. Merton made a mistake? " he said to himself. " She said it was a week's pay. But, of course, she wouldn't pay ten dollars for the little I am to do."

Luke decided that the extra sum was given him on account of the service he had already been fortunate enough to render the old lady.

It is not always wise to display money in a public conveyance. This was a lesson which Luke was destined to learn by an embarrassing experience.

Next to him sat rather a showily dressed woman, with keen, sharp eyes. She took notice of the bank-note which Luke drew from the envelope, and prepared to take advantage of the knowledge.

No sooner had Luke replaced the envelope in his pocket than this woman put her hand in hers, and,

after a pretended search, exclaimed, in a loud voice:
"There is a pickpocket in this car. I have been
robbed!"

Of course, this statement aroused the attention
of all the passengers.

"What have you lost, madam?" inquired an old
gentleman.

"A ten-dollar bill," answered the woman.

"Was it in your pocketbook?"

"No," she replied, glibly. "It was in an envelope. It was handed to me by my sister just before
I left home."

As soon as Luke heard this declaration, he understood that the woman had laid a trap for him, and
he realized his imprudence in displaying the
money. Naturally he looked excited and disturbed.
He saw that in all probability the woman's word
would be taken in preference to his. He might be
arrested, and find it difficult to prove his innocence.

"Have you any suspicion as to who took it?"
asked the old gentleman.

"I think this boy took it," said the woman, point-
ing to Luke.

Hostile and suspicious eyes were turned upon the
latter.

Why is it that people are prone to believe evil of
one who is accused, and to pronounce a verdict of
guilty on that account alone?

"It's terrible, and he so young!" said an old lady
with a severe cast of countenance, who sat next to

the old gentleman. "What is the world coming to?"

"What, indeed, ma'am?" echoed the old gentleman.

Luke felt that it was time for him to say something.

"This lady is quite mistaken," he declared, pale but resolute. "I'm no thief."

"It can easily be proved," said the woman, with a cunning smile. "Let the boy show the contents of his pockets."

"Yes, that is only fair."

Luke saw that his difficulties were increasing.

"I admit that I have a ten-dollar bill in an envelope," he said.

"I told you so!" cried the woman, triumphantly.

"But it is my own."

"Graceless boy!" said the old gentleman, severely. "Do not add falsehood to theft."

"I am speaking the truth, sir."

"How the boy brazens it out!" murmured the sour-visaged lady, who was an old maid, but not from choice.

"Return the lady her money, unless you wish to be arrested," said the old gentleman. "It is really shocking that so young a boy should be so unprincipled."

"I don't intend to give this person"—Luke found it hard to say lady—" what she has no claim to."

"Young man, you will find that you are making

a grand mistake. Probably if you give up the money the lady will not prosecute you."

" No, I will have pity upon his youth," said the woman.

" I can tell exactly where I got the money," went on Luke, desperately.

" Where did you get it? " asked the old maid, with a sarcastic smile.

" From Mrs. Merton, of Prairie Avenue."

" What did she give it to you for? "

" I am in her employment."

" Gentlemen," said the woman, shrugging her shoulders, " you can judge whether this is a probable story."

" I refer to Mrs. Merton herself," said Luke.

" No doubt! You want to gain time. Boy, I am getting out of patience. Give me my money! "

" I have no money of yours, madam," replied Luke, provoked; " and you know that as well as I do."

" So you are impertinent, as well as a thief," said the old gentleman. " I have no more pity for you. Madam, if you take my advice, you will have the lying rascal arrested."

" I would prefer that he should give up the money quietly."

" I will take it upon myself to call a policeman when the car stops. I have seldom seen a more hardened young villain."

" You do me great injustice, sir," said Luke.

" Why do you judge so severely of one whom you do not know? Why do you accept this person's word, and refuse to believe me?"

" Because, young man, I have lived too long to be easily deceived. I pride myself upon my judgment of faces, and I can see the guilt in yours."

The woman gazed about her triumphantly. It looked to her as if her trick would be successful, and she would gain ten dollars by sacrificing the reputation of a boy. I hope there are not many persons of either sex so contemptibly mean as was this well-dressed woman.

Luke looked about him earnestly.

" Is there no one in this car who believes me innocent?" he asked.

" No," said the old gentleman. " We all believe that this very respectable lady charges you justly."

" I say amen to that," added the old maid, nodding sharply.

When things are at the worst they are liable to take a turn.

Next to the old maid sat a man of about thirty-five, in a business suit, who, though he had said nothing, had listened attentively to the charges and counter-charges. In him Luke was to find a powerful and effective friend.

" Speak for yourself, old gentleman," he said. " You certainly are old enough to have learned a lesson of Christian charity."

"Sir," exclaimed the old gentleman, in a lofty tone, "I don't require any instruction from you."

"Why do you think the boy a thief? Did you see him take the money?"

"No, but its presence in his pocket is proof enough for me of his guilt."

"Of course it is!" said the old maid, triumphantly, and she glared at Luke's defender in a malevolent way.

The young man did not appear in the least disconcerted.

"I have seldom encountered more uncharitable people," he said. "You are ready to pronounce the boy guilty without any proof at all."

"Don't it occur to you that you are insulting the lady who brings the charge?" asked the old gentleman, sternly.

The young man laughed.

"The woman has brought a false charge," he said.

"Really, this is outrageous!" cried the old maid. "If I were in her place I would make you suffer for this calumny."

"Probably I know her better than you do. I am a salesman in Marshall Field's drygoods store, and this lady is a notorious shoplifter. She is varying her performances to-day. I have a great mind to call a policeman. She deserves arrest."

Had a bombshell exploded in the car, there would not have been a greater sensation. The woman rose without a word, and signaled to have the car stopped.

"Now, sir," went on the young man, sternly, "if you are a gentleman, you will apologize to this boy for your unworthy suspicions, and you, too, madam."

The old maid tossed her head, but could not find a word to say, while the old gentleman looked the picture of mortification.

"We are all liable to be mistaken!" he muttered, in a confused tone.

"Then be a little more careful next time, both of you! My boy, I congratulate you on your triumphant vindication."

"Thank you, sir, for it. I should have stood a very poor chance without your help."

The tide was turned, and the uncharitable pair found so many unfriendly glances fixed upon them that they were glad to leave the car at the next crossing.

CHAPTER XIII

TOM BROOKS IN TROUBLE

"I begin to think I am the favorite of fortune," thought Luke. "Ten dollars will more than pay a month's rent. Mother will feel easy now about her loss of employment."

Some boys would have felt like taking a holiday for the balance of the day, perhaps, or going to a place of amusement, but Luke bought his evening papers as usual. He had but half a dozen left when his new acquaintance, Stephen Webb, sauntered along.

"How's business, Luke?" he asked.

"Very fair, thank you."

"Give me a *News*."

Stephen passed over a penny in payment, but did not seem inclined to go away.

"I meant to see you before," he said, "but my time got filled up."

"Have you taken a situation, then?" asked Luke.

"No, I am still a man of leisure. Why don't you hire a small store, and do a general periodical business? It would pay you better."

"No doubt it would, but it would take money to open and stock such a store."

"I may make a proposition to you some time to go in with me, I furnishing the capital, and you managing the business."

"I am always open to a good offer," said Luke, smiling.

Stephen Webb's available capital was less than Luke's, but he wanted to create the impression that he was a man of means, and also to worm himself into the newsboy's confidence.

"I suppose I ought to have some business, but I'm a social kind of fellow, and should want a partner, a smart, enterprising, trustworthy person like you."

"Thank you for the compliment."

"Never mind that! I am a judge of human nature, and I felt confidence in you at once."

Somehow Luke was not altogether inclined to take Stephen Webb at his own valuation. His new acquaintance did not impress him as a reliable man of business, but he had no suspicion of anything underhand.

By this time Luke had disposed of his remaining papers.

"I am through for the day," he said, "and shall go home."

"Do you walk or ride?"

"I walk."

"If you don't mind, I will walk along with you. I haven't taken much exercise to-day."

Luke had no reason for declining this proposal,

and accepted Stephen's companionship. They walked on Clark Street to the bridge, and crossed the river. Presently they reached Milwaukee Avenue.

"Isn't the walk too long for you?" asked Luke.

"Oh, no! I can walk any distance when I have company. I shall take a car back."

Stephen accompanied the newsboy as far as his own door. He would like to have been invited up, but Luke did not care to give him such an invitation. Though Stephen seemed very friendly, he was not one with whom he cared to cultivate intimate relations.

"Well, so long!" said Stephen, with his "goodnight," "I shall probably see you to-morrow."

"I have found out where they live," thought Stephen. "On the whole, I am making a very good detective. I'll drop a line to Uncle Thomas this evening."

Meanwhile, Luke went upstairs two steps at a time. He was the bearer of good tidings, and that always quickens the steps.

He found his mother sitting in her rocking-chair with a sober face.

"Well, mother," he asked, gayly, "how have you passed the day?"

"Very unprofitably, Luke. I went out this afternoon, and visited two places where I thought they might have some sewing for me, but I only met with disappointment. Now that I have a sewing macnine, it is a great pity that I can't make use of it."

" Don't be troubled, mother! We can get along well enough."

" But we have only your earnings to depend upon, Luke."

" If I always have as good a day as this, we can depend on those very easily."

" Did you earn much, Luke?" asked Bennie.

" I earned a lot of money."

Mrs. Walton looked interested, and Luke's manner cheered her.

" There are always compensations, it seems. I was only thinking of my own bad luck."

" What do you say to that, mother?" and Luke displayed the ten-dollar bill.

" I don't understand how you could have taken in so much money, Luke."

" Then I will explain," and Luke told the story of the adventure on State Street, and his rescue of the old lady from the danger of being run over.

" The best of it is," he concluded, " I think I shall get regular employment for part of my time from Mrs. Merton. Whatever I do for her will be liberally paid for."

Luke went to a bakery for some cream cakes, of which Bennie was particularly fond, as an addition to their frugal supper, and the evening was passed in a very cheerful and hopeful fashion.

At the same time Stephen Webb was busily engaged in the writing room of the Palmer House, inditing a letter to his uncle. We will take the liberty of looking over his shoulder while he writes:

"DEAR UNCLE THOMAS: I have devoted my whole time to the task which you assigned me, and have met with very good success. I found the boy uncommunicative, and had to exert all my ingenuity."

Of the accuracy of this and other statements, the reader will judge for himself.

"The boy has a mother and a younger brother. They depend for support chiefly upon what he can earn, though the mother does a little sewing, but that doesn't bring in much. They live in Green Street, near Milwaukee Avenue. I have been there, and seen the house where they reside. It is a humble place, but as good, I presume, as they can afford. No doubt they are very poor, and have all they can do to make both ends meet.

"I have learned this much, but have had to work hard to do it. Of course, I need not say that I shall spare no pains to meet your expectations. If you should take me into your confidence, and give me an idea of what more you wish to know, I feel sure that I can manage to secure all needed information. Your dutiful nephew,

STEPHEN WEBB."

Thomas Browning, in his Milwaukee home, read this letter with satisfaction.

"My nephew seems curious," he said, meditatively; "but I do not feel disposed to tell him my object in looking up those Waltons. If he knew my secret he would be likely to trade upon it. That way of making a living would suit him better than solid work."

He wrote briefly to his nephew:

"You have done well thus far, and I appreciate your zeal. Get the boy to talking about his father, if you can. Let me hear anything he may say on this subject. As to my motive, I suspect that Mr. Walton may have been an early acquaintance of mine. If so, I may feel disposed to do something for the family."

"Uncle Thomas may tell that to the marines," said the astute Stephen. "He can't humbug me by posing as a philanthropist. He looks out for number one every time. I'll follow up this matter, and I may learn more in course of time."

On his way to the Sherman House, the next morning, Luke witnessed rather an exciting scene, in which his old friend, Tom Brooks, played a prominent part.

There was a Chinese laundry on Milwaukee Avenue kept by a couple of Chinamen who were peaceably disposed if not interfered with. But several

boys, headed by Tom Brooks, had repeatedly annoyed the laundrymen, and excited their resentment.

On this particular morning Tom sent a stone
crashing through the window of Ah King. The
latter had been on the watch, and, provoked beyond
self-control, rushed out into the street, wild with
rage, and pursued Tom with a flatiron in his hand.

" Help! help! murder!" exclaimed Tom, panic-
stricken, running away as fast as his legs would
carry him.

But anger, excited by the broken window, lent
wings to the Chinaman's feet, and he gained rapidly
upon the young aggressor.

CHAPTER XIV

Tom Brooks had reason to feel alarmed, for his Chinese pursuer was very much in earnest, and fully intended to strike Tom with the flatiron. Though this was utterly wrong, some excuse must be made for Ah King, who had frequently been annoyed by Tom.

It was at this critical juncture that Luke Walton appeared on the scene.

He had no reason to like Tom, but he instantly prepared to rescue him. Fortunately, he knew Ah King, whom he had more than once protected from the annoyance of the hoodlums of the neighborhood. Luke ran up and seized the Chinaman by the arm.

"What are you going to do?" he demanded, sternly.

"Fool boy bleak my window," said Ah King. "I bleak his head."

"No, you mustn't do that. The police will arrest you."

"Go 'way! Me killee white boy," cried Ah King, impatiently, trying to shake off Luke's grasp. "He bleak window—cost me a dollee."

87

" I'll see that he pays it, or is arrested," said
Luke.

Unwillingly Ah King suffered himself to be persuaded, more readily, perhaps, that Tom was now
at a safe distance.

" You plomise me? " said Ah King.

" Yes; if he don't pay, I will. Go and get the
window mended."

Luke easily overtook Tom, who was looking
round the corner to see how matters were going.

" Has he gone back? " asked Tom, rather anxiously.

" Yes, but if I hadn't come along, he would, perhaps, have killed you."

" You only say that to scare me," said Tom, uneasily.

" No, I don't; I mean it. Do you know how I
got you off? "

" How? "

" I told Ah King you would pay for the broken
window. It will cost a dollar."

" I didn't promise," said Tom, significantly.

" No," said Luke, sternly, " but if you don't do it,
I will myself have you arrested. I saw you throw
the stone at the window."

" What concern is it of yours? " asked Tom,
angrily. " Why do you meddle with my business? "

" If I hadn't meddled with your business, you
might have a fractured skull by this time. It is a

contemptibly mean thing to annoy a poor Chinaman."

"He's only a heathen."

"A well-behaved heathen is better than a Christian such as you are."

"I don't want any lectures," said Tom, in a sulky
tone.

"I presume not. I have nothing more to say
except that I expect you to hand me that dollar to-
night."

"I haven't got a dollar."

"Then you had better get one. I don't believe
you got a dollar's worth of sport in breaking the
window, and I advise you hereafter to spend your
money better."

"I don't believe I will pay it," said Tom, eying
Luke closely, to see if he were in earnest.

"Then I will report your case to the police."

"You're a mean fellow," said Tom, angrily.

"I begin to be sorry I interfered to save you.
However, take your choice. If necessary, I will
pay the dollar myself, for I have promised Ah
King; but I shall keep my word about having you
arrested."

It was a bitter pill for Tom to swallow, but he
managed to raise the money, and handed it to Luke
that evening. Instead of being grateful to the one
who had possibly saved his life, he was only the
more incensed against him, and longed for an opportunity to do him an injury.

" I hate that Luke Walton," he said to one of his
intimate friends. " He wants to boss me, and all
of us, but he can't do it. He's only fit to keep company with a heathen Chinee."

Luke spent but a couple of hours in selling
papers. He had not forgotten his engagement with
Mrs. Merton, and punctually at ten o'clock he
pulled the bell of the house in Prairie Avenue.

Just at that moment the door was opened, and
he faced a boy of his own age, a thin, dark-com-
plexioned youth, of haughty bearing. This, no
doubt, he concluded, was Harold Tracy.

" What do you want? " he asked, superciliously.

" I should like to see Mrs. Merton."

" Humph! What business have you with Mrs.
Merton? "

Luke was not favorably impressed with Harold's
manner, and did not propose to treat him with
the consideration which he evidently thought his
due.

" I come here at Mrs. Merton's request," he said,
briefly. " As to what business we have together,
I refer you to her."

" It strikes me that you are impudent," retorted
Harold, angrily.

" Your opinion of me is of no importance to me.
If you don't care to let Mrs. Merton know I am
here, I will ring again and ask the servant to do
so."

Here a lady, bearing a strong personal resemblance to Harold, made her appearance, entering the hall from the breakfast room in the rear.

"What is it, Harold?" she asked, in a tone of authority.

"Here is a boy who says he wants to see Aunt Eliza."

"What can he want with her?"

"I asked him, but he won't tell."

"I must trouble him to tell me," said Mrs. Tracy, closing her thin mouth with a snap.

"Like mother—like son," thought Luke.

"Do you hear?" demanded Mrs. Tracy, unpleasantly.

"I am here by Mrs. Merton's appointment, Mrs. Tracy," said Luke, firmly. "I shall be glad to have her informed that I have arrived."

"And who are you, may I ask?"

"Perhaps you've got your card about you?" sneered Harold.

"I have," answered Luke, quietly.

With a comical twinkle in his eye, he offered one to Harold.

"Luke Walton," repeated Harold.

"Yes, that is my name."

"I don't think my aunt will care to see you," said Mrs. Tracy, who was becoming more and more provoked with the "upstart boy," as she mentally termed him.

"Perhaps it would be better to let her know I am here."

" It is quite unnecessary. I will take the respon-
sibility."

Luke was quite in doubt as to what he ought to
do. He could not very well prevent Harold's
closing the door, in obedience to his mother's directions, but fortunately the matter was taken out of
his hands by the old lady herself, who, unobserved
by Harold and his mother, had been listening to
the conversation from the upper landing. When
she saw her visitor about to be turned out of the
house, she thought it quite time to interfere.

" Louisa," she called, in a tone of displeasure,
" you will oblige me by not meddling with my visi-
tors. Luke, come upstairs."

Luke could not forbear a smile of triumph as he
passed Harold and Mrs. Tracy, and noticed the look
of discomfiture on their faces.

" I didn't know he was your visitor, Aunt
Eliza," said Mrs. Tracy, trembling with the anger
she did not venture to display before her wealthy
relative.

" Didn't he say so?" asked Mrs. Merton,
sharply.

" Yes, but I was not sure that he was not an im-
postor."

" You had only to refer the matter to me, and
I could have settled the question. Luke is in my
employ——"

" In your employ?" repeated Mrs. Tracy, in surprise.

"Yes; he will do errands for me, and sometimes accompany me to the city."

"Why didn't you call on Harold? He would be very glad to be of service to you."

"Harold had other things to occupy him. I prefer the other arrangement. Luke, come into my room and I will give you directions."

Mrs. Tracy and Harold looked at each other as the old lady and Luke disappeared.

"This is a new freak of Aunt Eliza's," said Mrs. Tracy. "Why does she pass over you, and give the preference to this upstart boy?"

"I don't mind that, mother," replied Harold. "I don't want to be dancing attendance on an old woman."

"But she may take a fancy to this boy—she seems to have done so already—and give him part of the money that ought to be yours."

"If we find there is any danger of that, I guess we are smart enough to set her against him. Let her have the boy for a servant if she wishes."

"I don't know but you are right, Harold. We must be very discreet, for Aunt Eliza is worth half a million."

"And how old is she, mother?"

"Seventy-one."

"That's pretty old. She can't live many years."

"I hope she will live to a good old age," said Mrs. Tracy, hypocritically, "but when she dies. it is only fair that we should have her money."

CHAPTER XV

A WELCOME GIFT

When Luke and Mrs. Merton were alone, the old lady said, with a smile: "You seemed to have some difficulty in getting into the house."

"Yes," answered Luke. "I don't think your nephew likes me."

"Probably not. Both he and his mother are afraid someone will come between me and them. They are selfish, and cannot understand how I can have any other friends or beneficiaries. You are surprised that I speak so openly of such near relatives to such a comparative stranger. However, it is my nature to be outspoken. And now, Luke, if you don't think it will be tiresome to escort an old woman, I mean to take you downtown with me."

"I look upon you as a kind friend, Mrs. Merton," responded Luke, earnestly. "I want to thank you for the handsome present you made me yesterday. I didn't expect anything like ten dollars."

"You will find it acceptable, however, I don't doubt. Seriously, Luke, I don't think it's too much to pay for saving my life. Now, if you will wait here five minutes, I will be ready to go out with you."

Five minutes later Mrs. Merton came into the room attired for the street. They went downstairs together, and Luke and she got on board a street car.

They were observed by Mrs. Tracy and Harold as they left the house.

"Aunt Eliza's very easily imposed upon," remarked the latter.

"She scarcely knows anything of that boy, and she has taken him out with her. How does she know but he is a thief?"

"He looks like one," said Harold, in an amiable tone. "If aunt is robbed, I shan't pity her. She will deserve it."

"Very true; but you must remember that it will be our loss as well as hers. Her property will rightfully come to us, and if she is robbed we shall inherit so much the less."

"You're sharp, mother. I didn't think of that."

"I have been thinking, Harold, it may be well for you to find out something of this boy. If you can prove to Aunt Eliza that he is of bad character, she will send him adrift."

"I'll see about it, mother. I don't like him at all."

Meanwhile Mrs. Merton and Luke were on their way to the business portion of the city.

"I think I will stop at Adams Street, Luke," said the old lady. "I shall have to go to the Continental Bank. Do you know where it is?"

"I believe it is on La Salle Street, corner of Adams."

"Quite right. I shall introduce you to the paying teller as in my employ, as I may have occasion to send you there alone at times to deposit or draw money."

From where the cars left them the old lady walked with Luke to the bank.

"I wish Harold was more like you," she said. "His mother's suggestion that I should take him with me as an escort would be just as disagreeable to him as to me."

"Is he attending school?" asked Luke.

"Yes. He is preparing for college, but he is not fond of study, and I doubt whether he ever enters. I think he must be about your age."

"I am nearly sixteen."

"Then he is probably a little older."

They entered the bank, and Mrs. Merton, going to the window of the paying teller, presented a check for a hundred dollars.

"How will you have it, Mrs. Merton?" asked the teller.

"In fives and tens. By the way, Mr. Northrop, please take notice of this boy with me. I shall occasionally send him by himself to attend to my business. His name is Luke Walton."

"His face looks familiar. I think we have met before."

"I have sold you papers more than once, Mr.

Northrop," said Luke. "I stand on Clark Street,
near the Sherman."

"Yes, I remember, now. We bank officials are
apt to take notice of faces."

"Here, Luke, carry this money for me," said
Mrs. Merton, putting a lady's pocketbook into the
hand of her young escort. "You are less likely to
be robbed than I."

Luke was rather pleased at the full confidence
his new employer seemed to repose in him.

"I am now going up on State Street," said Mrs.
Merton, as they emerged into the street. "You
know the store of Marshall Field?"

"Oh, yes; everybody in Chicago knows that,"
said Luke.

"I am going there."

For a lady of her years, Mrs. Merton was a fair
walker. In a few minutes they stood before the
large store, and Mrs. Merton entered, followed by
Luke.

Mrs. Merton went to that part of the establishment where woolens are sold, and purchased a dress
pattern. To Luke's surprise, the salesman was the
same one who had come to his assistance in the car
the day previous when he was charged with stealing. The recognition was mutual,

"I believe we have met before," said the young
man, with a smile.

"Yes, fortunately for me," answered Luke, gratefully.

"The two parties who were determined to find you guilty looked foolish when they ascertained the real character of your accuser."

"What is this, Luke? You didn't tell me of it," said Mrs. Merton.

The story was related briefly.

"I should like to meet that woman," said Mrs. Merton, nodding energetically. "I'd give her a piece of my mind. Luke, you may hand me ten dollars."

The goods were wrapped up and the change returned.

"Where shall I send the bundle, Mrs. Merton?" asked the salesman, deferentially.

"Luke will take it."

As they left the store, Mrs. Merton said: "Did you think I was buying this dress for myself, Luke?"

"I thought so," Luke answered.

"No, I have dresses enough to last me a lifetime, I may almost say. This dress pattern is for your mother."

"For my mother?" repeated Luke, joyfully.

"Yes; I hope it will be welcome."

"Indeed it will. Mother hasn't had a new dress for over a year."

"Then I guessed right. Give it to her with my compliments, and tell her I give it to her for your sake. Now, I believe I will go home."

No present made to Luke could have given him

so much pleasure as this gift to his mother, for he knew how much she stood in need of it.

When they reached the house on Prairie Avenue, they met Mrs. Tracy on the steps. She had been out for a short call.

"Did you have a pleasant morning, Aunt Eliza?" she asked, quite ignoring Luke.

"Yes, quite so. Luke, I won't trouble you to come in. I shall not need you to-morrow. The next day you may call at the same hour."

Luke turned away, but was called back sharply by Mrs. Tracy.

"Boy," she said, "you are taking away my aunt's bundle. Bring it back directly."

"Louisa," said the old lady, "don't trouble yourself. That bundle is meant for Luke's mother."

"Something you bought for her?"

"Yes, a dress pattern."

"Oh!" sniffed Mrs. Tracy, eying Luke with strong disapproval. "Do you know anything about this boy?" she asked as they entered the house.

"Yes. Why?"

"I hope he won't impose upon you?"

"Thank you. I am not a child, Louisa."

"The boy looks artful."

"I can't say much for your discrimination."

"If anything happens, you will remember that I warned you."

"I shall remember," said the old lady, with an amused smile.

CHAPTER XVI

THOMAS BROWNING AT HOME

In one of the handsomest streets in Milwaukee stood a private residence which was quite in harmony with its surroundings. It looked like the home of a man of ample means. It was luxuriously furnished, and at one side was a conservatory. It was very apt to attract the attention of strangers, and the question was frequently asked: " Who lives there? "

And the answer would be: " Thomas Browning, one of our most prominent citizens. He will probably be mayor some day."

Yes, this was the residence of Thomas Browning, formerly Thomas Butler, the man to whom the dead father of Luke Walton had intrusted the sum of ten thousand dollars to carry to his wife and children. How he fulfilled his trust, or, rather, did not fulfill it, we already know. But in Milwaukee, where Mr. Browning had become a leading citizen, it was not known. It was entirely inconsistent with what was believed to be his character. For Mr. Browning was president of one charitable society and treasurer of another. At the annual meetings of these so-

cieues he was always called upon to spe..., and his
allusions to the poverty and privations of those who
were cared for by these societies never failed to
produce an impression.

"What a good man he is!" said many who
listened with sympathetic interest.

It was popularly supposed that he gave away
large sums in charity. Indeed, he admitted the fact,
but explained the absence of his name from sub-
scription papers by saying: "All my gifts are an-
onymous. Instead of giving my name, I prefer to put
down ' Cash,' so much, or ' A Friend,' such another
sum. I don't wish to influence others, but it jars
upon me to have my name ostentatiously paraded
in the public prints."

Now, in all subscriptions there are donations as-
cribed to " Cash " and " A Friend," and whenever
these occurred, it was generally supposed they rep-
resented Mr. Browning. But, to let the reader
into a little secret, this was only a shrewd device
of Mr. Browning's to have the reputation of a philanthropist at little or no expense, for, as a matter
of fact, he never contributed at all to the charities
in which he seemed to take such an interest!

In a pleasant room on the second floor sat the
pseudo-philanthropist. The room was furnished as
a library. At a writing table, poring over what
looked like an account book, he looked the picture
of comfort and respectability. A few well-chosen
engravings adorned the walls. A pleasant light

was diffused about the room from a chandelier sus-
pended over the table.

Thomas Browning leaned back in his chair, and
a placid smile overspread his naturally harsh features. He looked about him, and his thoughts
somehow ran back to a time when he was very
differently situated.

" Five years ago to-night," he said, " I was well-
nigh desperate. I hadn't a cent to bless myself
with, nor was the prospect of getting one particularly bright. How I lived, for a considerable time,
I hardly know. I did have a notion at one time,
when I was particularly down on my luck, of com-
mitting suicide, and so ending the struggle once
for all. It would have been a great mistake!" he
added after a pause. " I didn't foresee at the
time the prosperous years that lay before me.
Frederick Walton's money changed my whole life.
Ten thousand dollars isn't a fortune, but it proved
the basis of one. It enabled me to float the Excelsior Mine. I remember there were a hundred
thousand shares at two dollars a share, all based
upon a few acres of mining land which I bought
for a song. With the ten thousand dollars, I
hired an office, printed circulars, distributed glowing
accounts of imaginary wealth, etc. It cost considerable for advertising, but I sold seventy thousand
shares, and when I had gathered in the money I
let the bottom fall out. There was a great fuss, of
course, but I figured as the largest loser, being the

owner of thirty thousand shares (for which I hadn't paid a cent), and so shared the sympathy extended to losers. It was a nice scheme, and after deducting all expenses, I made a clean seventy-five thousand dollars out of it, which, added to my original capital, made eighty-five thousand. Then I came to Milwaukee and bought this house. From that time my career has been upward and onward. My friends say some day I shall be mayor of the city. Well, stranger things have happened, and who knows but my friends may be right!"

At this moment a servant entered the library.

"Well, Mary, what is it?" asked the philanthropist.

"Please, sir, there's a poor woman at the door, and she would like to see you."

"Ah, yes, she wants relief from the Widows' and Orphans' Society, probably. Well, send her up. I am always at home to the poor."

"What a good man he is!" thought Mary. "It's strange he gives such low wages to the girls that work for him. He says it's because he gives away so much money in charities."

Mary ushered in, a moment later, a woman in a faded dress, with a look of care and sorrow on her thin features.

"Take a seat, madam," said Thomas Browning, urbanely. "Did you wish to see me?"

"Yes, sir. I am in difficulties, and have ventured to call upon you."

"I am glad to see you.   I am always ready to see
the unfortunate."

"Yes, sir; I know you have the reputation of
being a philanthropist."

"No, no," said Mr. Browning, modestly. "Don't
mention it. I am fully aware of the flattering esti-
mation which is placed on my poor services, but
I really don't deserve it. It is, perhaps, as the
President of the Widows' and Orphans' Charitable
Society that you wish to speak to me."

"No, sir. It is as President of the Excelsior
Mining Company that I wish to make an appeal
to you."

"Oh!" ejaculated Browning, with a perceptible
change of countenance.

"Of course you remember it, sir. I was a
widow, with a small property of five thousand dollars left me by my late husband. It was all I had
on which to support myself and two children. The
banks paid poor interest, and I was in search of a
profitable investment. One of your circulars fell
into my hands. The shares were two dollars each,
and it was stated that they would probably yield
fifty per cent. dividends. That would support me
handsomely. But I didn't decide to invest until I
had written a private letter to you."

She took it from the pocket of her dress, and
offered it to Thomas Browning, but that gentleman waved it aside.

She continued: "You indorsed all that the circu-

tar contained. You said that within a year you
thought the shares would rise to at least ten dollars. So I invested all the money I had. You
know what followed. In six months the shares
went down to nothing, and I found myself penniless."

"I know it, my good woman," said Thomas
Browning. "I know it, to my cost. I myself had
sixty thousand dollars invested in the stock. I lost
it all."

"But you seem to be a rich man," said the
poor woman, looking about her.

"I have made it out of other ventures. But the
collapse of the mine was a sad blow to me. As
the president, I might have had something from the
wreck, but I did not. I suffered with the rest.
Now, may I ask what I can do for you?"

"It was on account of your advice that I bought
stock. Don't you think you ought to make up to
me a part of the loss?"

"Impossible!" said Browning, sharply. "Didn't
I tell you I lost much more heavily than you?"

"Then you can do nothing for me?"

"Yes; I can put you on the pension list of the
Widows' and Orphans' Society. That will entitle
you to receive a dollar a week for three months."

"I am not an object of charity, sir. I wish you
good-night."

"Good-night. If you change your mind come
to me."

"Very unreasonable, upon my word," soliloquized Thomas Browning. "As if I could afford to make up all the losses of stockholders. It would sweep off all I have."

At eleven o'clock Mr. Browning went to his bedchamber. He lit the gas and was preparing to disrobe, when his sharp ear detected the sound of suppressed breathing, and the point from which it proceeded. He walked quickly to the bed, bent over, and looked underneath. In an instant he had caught and pulled out, not over-gently, a man who had been concealed beneath it.

The intruder was a wretchedly dressed tramp. Browning allowed the man to get upon his feet, and then, facing him, demanded, sternly: "Why are you here? Did you come to rob me?"

CHAPTER XVII

A STRANGE VISITOR

"Did you come to rob me?" repeated Mr. Browning, as he stood facing the tramp, whom he had brought to the light from under the bed.

There was a strong contrast between the two men. One was a well-dressed, prosperous-looking gentleman, the other a man with a beard of a week's growth, disordered hair, and soiled garments.

There was an eager, questioning look on the face of the tramp, as he stared at the gentleman upon whose privacy he had intruded—not a look of fear, but a look of curiosity. Thomas Browning misinterpreted it. He thought the man was speechless from alarm, and rather enjoyed the thought that he had struck terror into the soul of the would-be burglar.

"Have you nothing to say for yourself?" demanded Browning, sternly.

The answer considerably surprised him.

"Why, pard, it's you, is it?" said the man, with the air of one to whom a mystery was made plain.

"What do you mean by your impertinence?" asked the respectable Mr. Browning, angrily.

"Well, that's a good one! Who'd have thought that this 'ere mansion belonged to my old friend and pard?"

"What do you mean? Are you crazy, fellow?"

"No, I ain't crazy, as I know of, but I'm flabbergasted—that's what I am."

"Have done with this trifling, and tell me why I shouldn't hand you over to the police?"

"I guess you won't do that, Tom Butler!" returned the burglar, coolly.

Browning stared in surprise and dismay at hearing his old name pronounced by this unsavory specimen of humanity.

"Who are you?" he demanded, quickly.

"Don't you know me?"

"No, I don't. I never saw you before. I don't associate with men of your class."

"Hear him now!" chuckled the tramp, in an amazed tone. "Why, Tom Butler, you an' me used to be pards. Don't you remember Jack King? Why, we've bunked together, and hunted for gold together, and almost starved together; but that was in the old days."

Browning looked the amazement he felt.

"Are you really Jack King?" he ejaculated, sinking back into an easy-chair, and staring hard at his unexpected visitor.

"I'm the same old coon, Tom, but I'm down at the heel, while you—do you really own this fine house, and these elegant fixin's?"

"Yes," answered Browning, mechanically.

"Well, you've fared better than I. I've been goin' down, down, till I've got about as far down as I can get."

"And you have become a burglar?"

"Well, a man must live, you know."

"You could work."

"Who would give such a lookin' man as I any work?"

"How did you get in?"

"That's my secret! You mustn't expect me to give myself away."

"And you had no idea whose house you were in?"

"I was told it belonged to a Mr. Browning."

"I am Mr. Browning—Thomas Browning."

"You! What has become of Butler?"

"I had good substantial reasons for changing my name—there was money in it, you understand."

"I'd like to change my own name on them terms. And now, Tom Butler, what are you going to do for me?"

Mr. Browning's face hardened. He felt no sympathy for the poor wretch with whom he had once been on terms of intimacy. He felt ashamed to think that they had ever been comrades, and he resented the tone of familiarity with which this outcast addressed him—a reputable citizen, a wealthy capitalist. a man whose name had been more than once mentioned in connection with the mayor's office.

"I'll tell you what I ought to do," he said, harshly.

"Well?"

"I ought to call a policeman, and give you in charge for entering my house as a burglar."

The tramp whistled, and eyed him keenly.

"You'd better not do that," he said without betraying alarm.

"Why not? Why should I not treat you like any other burglar?"

"Because—but I want to ask you a question," and the tramp, unbidden, sank into another easy-chair facing that of the owner of the mansion.

"What did you do with that money Walton gave you on his deathbed?"

A look of surprise and alarm overspread the countenance of Thomas Browning, a look which was not lost upon the tramp, who drew his own conclusions therefrom.

"What do you mean?" he faltered.

"Just what I say. What did you do with Walton's money?"

"I am at a loss to understand your meaning."

"No, you are not. However, I am ready to explain. On his deathbed Walton gave you ten thousand dollars to carry to his wife and family. Did you do it?"

"Who told you this?"

"It is unnecessary for me to say. It is enough that I know it. At the time you were poor enough. You might have had a few hundred dollars of your own, but certainly not much more. Now—it isn't so many years ago—I find you a rich man. Of course, I have my own ideas of how this came about."

"Do you mean to accuse me of dishonesty?" demanded Browning, angrily.

"I don't accuse you of anything. I am only thinking of what would be natural under the circumstances. I'm not an angel myself, Tom Butler, and I can't say but the money might have miscarried if it had been handed to me instead of to you. I wish it had; I wouldn't be the miserable-looking wretch I am now."

"Walton handed me some money," said Browning, cautiously—"not ten thousand dollars—and I handed it to his family."

"Where did they live?"

"In a country town," he answered, glibly.

Jack King eyed him shrewdly. He was a man of penetration, and he understood perfectly that Browning had appropriated the money for his own use.

"I was thinking I might run across Mrs. Walton some day," he said, significantly. "She would be glad to see me, as I knew her late husband in California."

"She is dead," said Browning, hastily.

" Dead! How long since! "

" She died soon after she heard of her husband's death. Died of grief, poor woman! "

" Were there no children? "

" Yes, there was a girl, but she was adopted by a relative in Massachusetts."

" I don't believe a word of it! " thought Jack King. " He wants to put me off the scent."

" Humph! And you gave the wife the money? "

" Of course."

" I may meet the girl some time; I might advertise for any of the family."

" Do you think they would be glad to see you? "

" They might help me, and I stand in need of help."

" There is no need of that. You are an old comrade in distress. I haven't forgotten the fact, though I pretended to, to try you. Here's a five-dollar bill. I'll let you out of the house myself. Considering how you entered it, you may count yourself lucky."

" That's all right, as far as it goes, Tom, but I want to remind you of a little debt you owe me. When you were out of luck at Murphy's diggings I lent you twenty-five dollars, which you have never paid back."

" I had forgotten it."

" I haven't. That money will come mighty convenient just now. It will buy me a better-looking suit, second-hand, and make a different man of me.

With it I can get a place and set up for a respectable human being."

"Here's the money," said Browning, reluctantly drawing the additional bills from his wallet. "Now that we are square, I hope you won't annoy me by further applications. I might have sent you out of the house under very different circumstances."

"You were always considerate, Tom," said the tramp, stowing away the bills in the pocket of his ragged vest. "May I refer to you if I apply for a situation?"

"Yes; but remember I am Thomas Browning. I prefer not to have it known that my name was ever Butler."

"All right! Now, if you'll do me the favor of showing me the door—I might scare a servant—I'll leave you to your slumbers."

"It's very awkward, that man's turning up," muttered Browning, as he returned from letting out his unsavory visitor. "How could he have heard about Walton's money?"

CHAPTER XVIII

HOW JACK KING FARED

Jack King left the house with the money Browning had unwillingly given him. He sought a cheap lodging, and the next morning proceeded to make himself respectable. When he had donned some clean linen, a suit of clothes which he bought cheap at a second-hand store, taken a bath, and called into requisition the services of a barber, it would have been hard to recognize him as the same man who had emerged from under the bed of the well-known philanthropist, a typical tramp and would-be burglar.

Jack King counted over the balance of his money, and found that he had nine dollars and thirty-seven cents left.

"This won't support me forever," he reflected. "I must get something to do."

While sauntering along, he fell in with an old acquaintance named Stone.

"What are you up to, King?" he asked.

"Looking for a job."

"You are my man, then. I am keeping a cigar store at the Prairie Hotel, but I have some business

calling me away from the city for six weeks or two
months. Will you take my place?"

"What are the inducements?"

"Board and lodging and five dollars a week."

"Agreed."

"Come over, then, and I will show you the place."

The hotel was a cheap one, not far from the rail-
way station, and though comfortable, was not pat-
ronized by fastidious travelers. Jack King looked
about him with satisfaction. To one who had been
only the day before outside the pale of respectability, it afforded a welcome refuge from poverty
and privation.

"When do you want me to take hold?" he asked.

"To-morrow."

"All right."

"Come around at ten o'clock. I want to leave
Milwaukee in the afternoon."

"There is great virtue in a respectable suit and
appearance," thought Jack King. "If Stone had
met me yesterday he would have steered clear of
me. Now that I have got my foot on the ladder
of respectability I will mount higher, if I can."

King could not help reflecting about the extraordinary prosperity of his old comrade, Tom
Butler, now Thomas Browning, Esq.

"What does it mean and how has it come
about?" he asked himself. "He seemed very uneasy when I asked him about Walton's money. I
believe he kept it himself. I wish I knew. If I

could prove it, it would be a gold mine for me. I must make inquiries, and, if, possible, find out Walton's family."

" Do you know anything of Thomas Browning?" he asked Stone.

" The philanthropist? Yes. What of him? "

" I called on him last evening."

Jack did not think it best to mention the circumstances of his visit.

" Indeed! How did you know him? "

" In California."

" I suppose he laid the foundation of his fortune there."

" Is he so rich, then? "

" Yes, probably worth a quarter of a million."

This was an exaggeration, but rich men's wealth is generally overstated.

" How does he stand in the city? "

" First-class. He has been mentioned for mayor. I shouldn't be surprised if he might get the office some day."

" He has certainly been very lucky," remarked King, quietly.

" I should say so. Was he rich in California? "

" Not when I knew him. At one time there he had to borrow money of me. He paid me back last evening."

" He is on the top of the ladder now, at any rate."

" His respectability would suffer a little," thought Jack King, " if I could prove that he had appropriated Walton's money. I must think the matter over, and secure some information if I can."

The next Sunday evening he called at the house of the philanthropist, and sent in his name.

Thomas Browning went himself to the door. He was afraid King might be wearing the same disreputable suit in which he had made his former visit. But to his relief his visitor looked quite respectable.

"Do you wish to see me?" he asked.

"Yes; but only for a social call. I am not acquainted in Milwaukee, and it does me good to see an old friend and comrade."

"I have not much time to spare, but come in!"

They went into the philanthropist's library, formerly described.

"Have you found anything to do?" asked Browning.

"Yes."

"What is it?"

King answered the question.

"It is not much," he added, "but will do for the present."

"At any rate, it is considerably better than entering a house at night and hiding under the bed," said Browning, dryly.

"So it is," answered King, smiling. "You must make allowance for my destitute condition. I little thought that I was in the house of an old friend.

I have been asking about you, Tom Butler—I beg pardon, Mr. Browning—and I find that you stand very high in Milwaukee."

A shade of annoyance showed itself on the philanthropist's face when King referred to him under his former name, but when his high standing was referred to he smiled complacently.

"Yes," he said, "I have been fortunate enough to win the good opinion of my fellow-citizens."

"Someone told me that you would probably run for mayor some day."

"It may be. I have been sounded on the subject."

"The worst of running for office is that if a man has ever done anything discreditable it is sure to be brought out against him."

"I hope you don't mean to imply that I have ever done anything discreditable," said Browning, sharply.

"Oh, dear, no! How could I think such a thing? But sometimes false charges are brought. If you had ever betrayed a trust, or kept money belonging to another, of course it would hurt you."

"Certainly it would," said the philanthropist, his voice betraying some nervousness, "but I am glad to say that my conscience is clear on that point. I must conciliate this fellow, or he may do me some harm," he thought. "I wonder whether he means anything?

"By the way, Jack, let me send for a bottle of

wine," he added, aloud. "We'll drink to the memory of old times."

"With all my heart, Tom. I see you're the right
sort. When you are nominated for office I will
work for you."

Browning smiled graciously on his visitor, and
the interview closed pleasantly.

"He's afraid of me!" thought Jack, as he left
the house. "There's something in that Walton
affair that he wants to hush up. It will take more
than a glass of wine to buy me off."

CHAPTER XIX

A SENSATIONAL INCIDENT

When Luke brought home the dress pattern his mother was much pleased.

"I have needed a dress for a good while," she said, "but I never felt that I could spare the money to buy even a common one. This material is very nice."

"It cost seventy-five cents a yard. I was with Mrs. Merton when she bought it."

"I hope you didn't hint to Mrs. Merton that I needed one."

"No, that isn't like me, mother, but I own that I was very glad when she thought of it."

"Please tell her how grateful I am."

"I will certainly do so. Now, mother, I want you to have it made up at once. I can spare the money necessary."

"It will cost very little. I will have it cut by a dressmaker and make it up myself. I hope you will long retain the friendship of Mrs. Merton."

"It won't be my fault if I don't. But I can't help seeing that her niece, Mrs. Tracy, and Harold, a boy about my age, look upon me with dislike."

"Why should they? I don't see how anyone can dislike you."

"You are my mother and are prejudiced in my favor. But I am sure they have no reason to dislike me. I think, however, they are jealous, and fear the old lady will look upon me with too much favor. She is very rich, I hear, and they expect to inherit all her fortune."

"Money makes people mean and unjust."

"If I can only get hold of some, I'll run the risk of that," said Luke. "I should feel a good deal more comfortable if I hadn't two enemies in the house. I am afraid they will try to set the old lady against me."

"Do your duty, my son, and leave the rest to God. It isn't well to borrow trouble."

"No doubt you are right, mother. I will follow your advice."

The next morning Luke was at his usual stand near the Sherman House when a boy who was passing uttered a slight exclamation of surprise. Looking up, Luke recognized Harold Tracy.

"So it's you, is it?" said Harold, not over politely.

"Yes," answered Luke. "I hope you are well."

"I didn't know you were a newsboy."

"I spend a part of my time in selling papers."

"Does Mrs. Merton know you are a newsboy?"

"I think I have told her, but I am not certain."

"It must be inconvenient for you to come so far as our house every day?"

"Of course it takes up some time, but Mrs. Merton does not allow me to work for nothing."

"How much does Aunt Eliza pay you?" asked Harold, his face showing the curiosity he felt.

"I would rather you would ask Mrs. Merton. I am not sure that she would care to have me tell."

"You seem to forget that I am her nephew—that is, her grandnephew. It is hardly likely she would keep such a thing secret from me."

"That may be, but I would rather you would ask her."

"Does she pay you more than two dollars a week?"

"Again I must refer you to her."

"It is ridiculous to make a secret of such a trifle," said Harold, annoyed.

Luke did not feel bound to make any reply, and Harold's curiosity manifested itself in another way.

"How much do you make selling papers?" he asked.

"I averaged about seventy-five cents a day before I began to work for Mrs. Merton. Now I don't make as much."

"Why don't you black boots, too? Many of the newsboys do."

"I never cared to take up that business."

"If you should go into it, I would give you a job now and then."

"I am not likely to go into that business, but I shall be glad to sell you a paper whenever you need one."

"You are not too proud to black boots, are you?" persisted Harold.

"I don't think it necessary to answer that question. I have always got along without it so far."

Harold carried the news home to his mother that Luke was a newsboy, and Mrs. Tracy found an opportunity to mention it at the supper table.

"Harold saw your paragon this morning, Aunt Eliza," she commenced.

"Have I a paragon? I really wasn't aware of it," returned the old lady.

"Your errand boy."

"Oh, Luke. Where did you see him, Harold?"

"He was selling papers near the Sherman House."

"I hope you bought one of him."

"I didn't have any change."

"Did you know he was a newsboy, Aunt Eliza?" asked Mrs. Tracy.

"Yes; he told me so. You speak of it as if it were something to his discredit."

"It is a low business, of course."

"Why is it a low business?"

"Oh, well, of course it is only poor street boys who engage in it."

"I am aware that Luke is poor, and that he has to contribute to the support of his mother and

brother. I hope, if you were poor, that Harold
would be willing to work for you."

"I wouldn't sell papers," put in Harold, decidedly.

"I don't suppose Luke sells papers from choice."

"Aunt Eliza, I don't see why you should so per-
sistently compare Harold with that ragged errand
boy of yours."

"Is he ragged? I am glad you noticed it. I must
help him to a new suit."

This was far from a welcome suggestion to Mrs.
Tracy, and she made haste to add: "I don't think
he's ragged. He dresses well enough for his position in life."

"Still, I think he needs some new clothes, and I
thank you for suggesting it, Louisa."

"What a provoking woman Aunt Eliza is!" said
Mrs. Tracy to herself. "Sometimes I wish I could
slap her, she is so contrary and perverse."

The next day, Luke, to his surprise, was asked to
accompany Mrs. Merton to a ready-made clothing
house on Clark Street, where he was presented with
a fine suit, costing twenty dollars.

"How kind you are, Mrs. Merton!" said Luke.

"I didn't notice that you needed a new suit," returned the old lady, "but my niece, Mrs. Tracy,
spoke of it, and I was glad to take the hint."

Luke was more astonished than ever. Was it
possible that Mrs. Tracy, who, he supposed, disliked
him, should so have interested herself in his behalf?

·It was hard to believe. There was a smile on Mrs. Merton's face that strengthened his incredulity, and he refrained from expressing his thanks to Mrs. Tracy when he met her.

It was in the afternoon of the same day that Luke, having an errand that carried him near the lake shore, strolled to the end of North Pier. He was fond of the water, but seldom had an opportunity to go out on it.

"How are you, Luke?" said a boy in a flat-bottomed boat a few rods away.

In the boy who hailed him Luke recognized John Hagan, an acquaintance of about his own age.

"Won't you come aboard?" asked John.

"I don't mind, if you'll come near enough."

In five minutes Luke found himself on board the boat. He took the oars and relieved John, who was disposed to rest.

They rowed hither and thither, never very far from the pier. Not far away was a boat of the same build, occupied by a man of middle size, whose eccentric actions attracted their attention. Now he would take the oars and row with feverish haste, nearly fifty strokes to a minute; then he would let his oars trail, and seem wrapped in thought. Suddenly the boys were startled to see him spring to his feet and, flinging up his arms, leap head first into the lake.

CHAPTER XX

AMBROSE KEAN'S IMPRUDENCE

Luke and his companion were startled by the sudden attempt at suicide, and for an instant sat motionless in their boat. Luke was the first to regain his self-possession.

"Quick, let us try to save him," he called to John Hagan.

They plunged their oars into the water, and the boat bounded over the waves. Fortunately they were but half a dozen rods from the place where the would-be suicide was now struggling to keep himself up. For, as frequently happens, when he actually found himself in the water, the instinct of self-preservation impelled the would-be self-destroyer to attempt to save himself. He could swim a very little, but the waters of the lake were in lively motion, his boat had floated away, and he would inevitably have drowned but for the energetic action of Luke and John. They swept their boat alongside, and Luke thrust his oar in the direction of the struggling man.

"Take hold of it," he said, "and we will tow you to your own boat."

Guided and sustained by the oar, the man gripped

the side of Luke's boat, leaving the oar free. His weight nearly overbalanced the craft, but with considerable difficulty the boys succeeded in reaching the other boat, and, though considerably exhausted, its late occupant managed to get in.

As he took his place in the boat he presented a sorry spectacle, for his clothes were wet through and dripping.

"You will take your death of cold unless you go on shore at once," said Luke.

"It wouldn't matter much if I did," said the young man, gloomily.

"We will row to shore also," said Luke to John Hagan. "He may make another attempt to drown himself. I will see what I can do to reason him out of it."

They were soon at the pier, and the three landed.

"Where do you live?" asked Luke, taking his position beside the young man.

The latter named a number on Vine Street. It was at a considerable distance, and time was precious, for the young man was trembling from the effects of his immersion.

"There is no time to lose. We must take a carriage," said Luke.

He summoned one, which fortunately had just returned from the pier, to which it had conveyed a passenger, and the two jumped in. The young man lay back in his seat, and remained sad and silent.

Luke helped him up to his room, a small one on

the third floor, and remained until he had changed his clothes and was reclining on the bed.

"You ought to have some hot drink," he said. "Can any be got in the house?"

"Yes; Mrs. Woods, the landlady, will have some hot water."

Luke went downstairs and succeeded in enlisting the sympathetic assistance of the kind-hearted woman by representing that her lodger had been upset in the lake and was in danger of a severe cold.

When the patient had taken down a cup of hot drink, he turned to Luke and said: "How can I thank you for your kindness?"

"There is no need to thank me. I am glad I was at hand when you needed me."

"What is your name?"

"Luke Walton."

"Mine is Ambrose Kean. You must think I am a fool."

"I think," said Luke, gently, "that you have some cause of unhappiness."

"You are right there. I have been unfortunate, but I am also an offender against the law, and it was the fear of exposure and arrest that made me take the step I did. I thought I was ready to die, but when I found myself in the water life seemed dearer than it had before, and I tried to escape. Thanks to you, I am alive, but now I almost wish that I had succeeded. I don't know how to face what is before me."

" Would you mind telling me what it is? "

" No; I need someone to confide in, and you deserve my confidence. Let me tell you, then, that I am employed in an office on Dearborn Street. My pay is small, twelve dollars a week, but it would be enough to support me if I had only myself to look out for. But I have a mother in Milwaukee, and I have been in the habit of sending her four dollars a week. That left me only eight dollars, which I found it hard to live on, and there was nothing left for clothes."

" I can easily believe that," said Luke.

" I struggled along, however, as best I might, but last week I received a letter from my mother saying that she was sick. Of course her expenses were increased, and she wrote to know if I could send her a little extra money. I have been living so close up to my income that I absolutely had less than a dollar in my pocket. Unfortunately, temptation came at a time when I was least prepared to resist it. One of our customers from the country came in when I was alone, and paid me fifty dollars in bills, for which I gave him a receipt. No one saw the payment made. It flashed upon me that this sum would make my mother comfortable even if her sickness lasted a considerable time. Without taking time to think, I went to an express office, and forwarded to her a package containing the bills. It started yesterday, and by this time is in my mother's hands. You see the situation I am placed in. The one who paid the money may come to the office at any time and reveal my guilt."

"I don't wonder that you were dispirited," returned Luke. "But can nothing be done? Can you not replace the money in time?"

"How can I? I have told you how small my salary is."

"Have you no friend or friends from whom you could borrow the money?"

"I know of none. I have few friends, and such as they are, are, like myself, dependent on small pay. I must tell you, by the way, how we became so poor. My mother had a few thousand dollars, which, added to my earnings, would have made us comparatively independent, but in an evil hour she invested them in a California mine, on the strength of the indorsement of a well-known financier of Milwaukee, Mr. Thomas Browning——"

"Who?" asked Luke, in surprise.

"Thomas Browning. Do you know him?"

"I have seen him. He sometimes comes to Chicago, and stops at the Sherman House."

"He recommended the stock so highly—in fact, he was the president of the company that put it on the market—that my poor mother thought it all right, and invested all she had. The stock was two dollars a share. Now it would not fetch two cents. This it was that reduced us to such extreme poverty."

"Do you think Mr. Browning was honest in his

recommendation of the mine?" asked Luke,
thoughtfully.

"I don't know. He claimed to be the principal
loser himself. But it is rather remarkable that he
is living like a rich man now. Hundreds lost their
money through this mine. As Mr. Browning had
himself been in California——"

"What is that?" asked Luke, in excitement.
"You say this Browning was once in California?
Can you tell when?"

"Half a dozen years ago, more or less."

"And he looks like the man to whom my poor
father confided ten thousand dollars for us," thought
Luke. "It is very strange. Everything tallies but
the name. The wretch who swindled us was named
Butler."

"Why do you ask when Mr. Browning was in
California?" asked the young man.

"Because my father died in California," answered
Luke, evasively, "and I thought it possible that Mr.
Browning might have met him."

CHAPTER XXI

A FRIEND IN NEED

"Mr. Browning is a man of very peculiar appearance," said Kean.

"You refer to the wart on the upper part of his right cheek?"

"Yes, it gives him a repulsive look."

"And yet he is popular in Milwaukee?"

"Yes, among those who were not swindled by his mining scheme. He has the reputation of a philanthropist, but I think it is more on account of what he says than what he does. He has done more harm than he can ever repair. For instance," added the young man, bitterly, "this crime which I have committed—I will call it by its right name—I was impelled to do by my mother's poverty, brought on by him."

"How does it happen that you are not at the office to-day?"

"I felt sick—sick at heart, rather than sick in body, and I sent word to my employer that I could not be there. I dread entering the office, for at any time exposure may come."

"If you could only raise the fifty dollars, you

could replace the money before it was inquired
for."

Ambrose Kean shook his head.

" I can't possibly raise it," he said, despondently.

" I would let you have it if I possessed as much
money, but, as you may suppose, I am poor."

" I am no less grateful to you, Luke. You have
a good heart, I am sure. You don't despise me?"

" No, why should I?"

" I have been guilty of a crime."

" But you are sorry for it. Is there positively no
one with whom you are acquainted who is rich
enough to help you?"

" There is one lady in Chicago—a rich lady—who
was a schoolmate of my mother. She was older
and in better circumstances, but they were good
friends."

" Who is this lady?"

" A Mrs. Merton."

" Mrs. Merton!" exclaimed Luke, in excitement.
" Of Prairie Avenue?"

" Yes; I believe she lives there."

" Why, I know her—I am in her employ," said
Luke.

Ambrose Kean stared at Luke in undisguised
amazement.

" Is this true?" he asked.

" Yes."

" Is she a kind lady? Do you think she would
help me in this trouble of mine?"

"She is very kind-hearted, as I know from my own experience. I will go to her at once, and see what I can do."

Ambrose Kean grasped Luke's hand with fervor.

"You are a friend sent from heaven, I truly believe," he said. "You have given me a hope of retrieving myself."

"I will leave you for a time," said Luke. "There is no time to be lost."

"I shall be full of anxiety till I see you again."

"Be hopeful. I think I shall bring you good news."

When Luke reached the house on Prairie Avenue he was about to ring the bell when Harold Tracy opened the door.

"You here again!" he said, in a tone of displeasure. "Weren't you here this morning?"

"Yes."

"Did Aunt Eliza ask you to come this afternoon?"

"No."

"Then what brings you?"

"Business," answered Luke, curtly, and he quietly entered the hall, and said to a servant who was passing through, "Will you be kind enough to ask Mrs. Merton if she will see me?"

"Well, you're cheeky!" ejaculated Harold, who had intended to keep him out.

"As long as Mrs. Merton doesn't think so, I shall not trouble myself," said Luke, coldly.

'Sooner or later Aunt Eliza will see you in your true colors," said Harold, provoked.

" I think she does now."

At this moment the servant returned.

" You are to go upstairs," she said. " Mrs. Merton will see you."

The old lady was sitting back in an easy-chair when Luke entered. She smiled pleasantly.

"This is an unexpected pleasure," she said—
" this afternoon call."

" I will tell you at once what brought me, Mrs. Merton."

" It isn't sickness at home, I hope? "

" No, I came for a comparative stranger."

Then Luke told the story of Ambrose Kean, his sudden yielding to temptation, his repentance and remorse.

" I am interested in your friend," said Mrs. Merton. " You say he appropriated fifty dollars? "

" Yes, but it was to help his mother."

" True, but it was a dangerous step to take. It won't be considered a valid excuse."

" He realizes all that. His employer is a just but strict man, and if the theft is discovered Kean will be arrested, and, of course, convicted."

" And you think I will help him? Is that why you have come to me with this story? "

" I don't think I would have done so if he had not mentioned you as an old friend and schoolmate of his mother."

"What's that?" added Mrs. Merton, quickly.
"His mother an old schoolmate of mine?"

"That is what he says."

"What was her name—before marriage?"

"Mary Robinson."

"You don't say so!" Mrs. Merton exclaimed
with vivacity. "Why, Mary was my favorite at
school. And this young man is her son?

"I would have helped him without knowing this,
but now I won't hesitate a moment. Mary's boy!
You must bring him here. I want to question him
about her."

"I can tell you something about her. She lost
her money by investing in a California mine—I
think it was the Excelsior Mine."

"She, too?"

Luke looked surprised. He did not understand
the meaning of this exclamation.

"I have a thousand shares of that worthless stock
myself," continued the old lady. "It cost me two
thousand dollars, and now it is worth nothing."

"The one who introduced the stock was a Mr.
Browning, of Milwaukee."

"I know. He was an unscrupulous knave, I have
no doubt. I could afford the loss, but hundreds invested, like poor Mary, who were ruined. Is the
man living, do you know?"

"Yes, he is living in Milwaukee. He is rich,
and is prominently spoken of as a candidate for
mayor."

"If he is ever a candidate I will take care that his connection with this swindling transaction is made known. A man who builds up a fortune on the losses of the poor is a contemptible wretch, in my opinion."

"And mine, too," said Luke. "It is very strange that he answers the description of a man who cheated our family out of ten thousand dollars."

"Indeed! How was that?"

Luke told the story, and Mrs. Merton listened with great interest.

"So all corresponds except the name?"

"Yes."

"He may have changed his name."

"I have thought of that. I mean to find out some time."

"I won't keep you any longer. Your friend is, no doubt, in great anxiety. I have the money here in bills. I will give them to you for him."

Mrs. Merton was in the act of handing a roll of bills to Luke when the door opened suddenly, and Mrs. Tracy entered.

She frowned in surprise and displeasure when she saw her aunt giving money to "that boy," as she contemptuously called him.

CHAPTER XXII

HOW AMBROSE KEAN WAS SAVED

"I didn't know you were occupied, Aunt Eliza," said Mrs. Tracy, in a significant tone, as she paused at the door.

"My business is not private," returned the old lady. "Come in, Louisa."

Mrs. Tracy did come in, but she regarded Luke with a hostile and suspicious glance.

"That is all, Luke," said his patroness. "You may go. You can report to me to-morrow."

"All right, ma'am."

When Luke had left the room, Mrs. Tracy said: "You appear to repose a great deal of confidence in that boy."

"Yes; I think he deserves it."

Mrs. Tracy coughed.

"You seem to trust him with a great deal of money."

"Yes."

"Of course, I don't want to interfere, but I think you will need to be on your guard. He is evidently bent on getting all he can out of you."

"That is vour judgment, is it, Louisa?"

138

"Yes, Aunt Eliza, since you ask me."

"He has done me a service this morning. He has brought to my notice a son of one of my old schoolmates who is in a strait, and I have sent him fifty dollars."

"By that boy?"

"Yes. Why not?"

"Are you sure the person to whom you sent the money will ever get it?"

"Please speak out what you mean. Don't hint. I hate hints."

"In plain terms, then, I think the boy will keep the money himself, or, at any rate, a part of it."

"I don't fear it."

"No fool like an old fool!" thought Mrs. Tracy, but she was too prudent to say it. She only coughed.

"You appear to have a bad cough, Louisa. Let me recommend you to take some of my cough medicine," said the old lady, with an amused look.

"Thank you, Aunt Eliza. I don't need it."

"Have you any more to say?"

"Nothing, except to warn you against that designing boy."

"You are very kind, Louisa, but I am not quite a simpleton. I have seen something of the world, and I don't think I am easily taken in. Now I propose to lie down for an hour. Afterwards I shall be glad to see you, if you wish an interview."

Mrs. Tracy left the room, not very well satisfied.

She really thought Luke had designs upon the old lady's money, and was averse even to his receiving a legacy, since it would take so much from Harold and herself.

"Harold, when I entered your aunt's room, what do you think I saw?"

This she said to Harold, who was waiting below.

"I don't know."

"Aunt Eliza was giving money to that boy."

"Do you know how much?"

"Fifty dollars."

"Whew! Was it for himself?"

"He came to her with a trumped-up story of an old schoolmate of aunt's who was in need of money."

"Do you think he will keep it himself?"

"I am afraid so."

"What a cheeky young rascal he is, to be sure! I have no doubt you are right."

"Yes; there is too much reason to think he is an unscrupulous adventurer, young as he is."

"Why don't you tell aunt so?"

"I have."

"And what does she say?"

"It doesn't make the least impression upon her."

"What do you think the boy will do?"

"Get her to make a will in his favor, or at least to leave him a large legacy."

Harold turned pale.

"That would be robbing us," he said.

"Of course it would. He wouldn't mind that, you know."

"He was very impertinent to me this morning."

"I presume so. He depends upon his favor with aunt."

"Isn't there anything we can do, mother?"

"I must consider."

Meanwhile Luke returned at once to the room of Ambrose Kean. He found the young man awaiting him with great anxiety.

"What success?" he asked, quickly.

"I have got the fifty dollars," answered Luke.

"Thank God! I am saved!" ejaculated the young man.

"Would you mind taking it round to the office with a note from me?" asked Kean.

"I will do so cheerfully."

"Then I shall feel at ease."

"Mrs. Merton would like to have you call on her. She remembered your mother at once."

"I shall be glad to do so, but shall be ashamed to meet her now that she knows of my yielding to temptation."

"You need not mind that. She also suffered from the rascality of Thomas Browning, and she will make allowances for you."

"Then I will go some day with you."

"You had better give me a letter to take to your employer with the money."

"I will"

Ambrose Kean wrote the following note:

"JAMES COOPER:

"DEAR SIR: Hiram Crossley called at the office yesterday and paid in fifty dollars due to you. Being busy, I thrust it into my pocket, and inadvertently took it with me. I think I shall be able to be at the office to-morrow, but think it best to send the money by a young friend. I gave Mr. Crossley a receipt. Yours respectfully,

"AMBROSE KEAN."

When Luke reached the office, Mr. Cooper was conversing with a stout, broad-shouldered man, of middle age, and Luke could not help hearing some of their conversation.

"You say you paid fifty dollars to my clerk, Mr. Crossley?" said the merchant.

"Yes."

"Have you his receipt?"

"Here it is."

Mr. Cooper examined it.

"Yes, that is his signature."

"Isn't he here to-day?"

"No; he sent word that he had a headache."

"And you don't find the money?"

"No."

"That is singular." And the two men exchanged glances of suspicion.

"What sort of a young man is he?"

"I never had any cause to suspect him."

"I hope it is all right."

"If it isn't, I will discharge him," said Cooper, nodding emphatically.

"He probably didn't think I would be here so soon. I didn't expect to be, but a telegram summoned me to the city on other business."

Of course Luke understood that the conversation related to Kean, and that he had arrived none too soon. He came forward.

"I have a letter for you from Mr. Kean," he said.

"Ha! Give it to me!"

Mr. Cooper tore open the envelope, saw the bank bills, and read the letter.

"It's all right, Mr. Crossley," he said, his brow clearing. "Read that letter."

"I am really glad," said Crossley.

"How is Mr. Kean?" asked Cooper, in a friendly tone.

"He had a severe headache, but he is better, and hopes to be at the office to-morrow."

"Tell him I shall be glad to see him, but don't want him to come unless he is really able."

"Thank you, sir. I will do so." And Luke left the office.

"It was a narrow escape," he said to himself. "Whenever I am tempted to be dishonest I will remember it."

He went back to Ambrose Kean, and told him what had happened at the office.

" I have escaped better than I deserved," he said.
" It will be a lesson to me. Please tell Mrs. Merton that her timely aid has saved my reputation and rescued my poor mother from sorrow and destitution."

" I will, and I am sure she will consider the money well spent."

The next morning, as Luke stood at his usual post, he saw Thomas Browning, of Milwaukee, come out of the Sherman House. He knew him at once by the wart on the upper part of his right cheek, which gave him a remarkable appearance.

" Can there be two persons answering this description? " Luke asked himself.

Thomas Browning came across the street, and paused in front of Luke.

CHAPTER XXIII

STEPHEN WEBB IS PUZZLED

" Will you have a morning paper? " asked Luke.

He wanted to have a few words with Mr. Browning, even upon an indifferent subject, as he now thought it probable that this was the man who had defrauded his mother and himself.

Browning, too, on his part, wished for an opportunity to speak with the son of the man he had so shamefully swindled. Though he had no reason to think that Luke or his mother had any knowledge of the trust, he felt a vague sense of uneasiness lest it should some day come out, and he be forced to disgorge the money with accumulated interest.

" Yes," he said, abruptly, " you may give me the *Times.*"

When the paper had been paid for, he said:

" Do you make a good living at selling papers? "

" It gives me about seventy-five cents a day," answered Luke.

" You can live on that, I suppose? "

" I have a mother to support."

" That makes a difference. Why do you stay in Chicago? You could make a better living farther West."

"In California?" asked Luke, looking intently at Browning.

Thomas Browning started.

"What put California into your head?" he asked.

"My father died in California."

"A good reason for your not going there."

"I thought you might be able to tell me something about California," continued Luke.

"Why should I?"

"I thought perhaps you had been there."

"You are right," said Browning, after a pause. "I made a brief trip to San Francisco at one time. It was on a slight matter of business. But I don't know much about the interior and can't give you advice."

"I wonder if this is true," thought Luke. "He admits having been to California, but says he has never been in the interior. If that is the case, he can't have met my father."

"I may at some time have it in my power to find you a place farther West, but not in California," resumed Browning. "I will take it into consideration. I frequently come to Chicago, and I presume you are to be found here."

"Yes, sir."

Thomas Browning waved his hand by way of good-by, and continued on his way.

"The boy seems sharp," he said to himself. "If he had the slightest hint of my connection with his father's money, he looks as if he would follow it up. Luckily there is no witness and no evidence. No one can prove that I received the money."

At the corner of Adams Street Mr. Browning encountered his nephew, Stephen Webb, who was gazing in at a window with a cigar in his mouth, looking the very image of independent leisure.

"You are profitably employed," said Browning, dryly.

Stephen Webb wheeled round quickly.

"Glad to see you, Uncle Thomas," he said, effusively. "I suppose you received my letter?"

"Yes."

"I hope you are satisfied. I had hard work to find out about the boy."

"Humph! I don't see how there could be anything difficult about it. I hope you didn't mention my name?"

"No. I suppose you are interested in the boy," said Stephen, with a look of curious inquiry.

"Yes; I always feel interested in the poor, and those who require assistance."

Browning's tone was that of the professional philanthropist.

"I am glad of that, uncle, for you have a poor nephew."

"And a lazy one," said Browning, sharply. "Where would I be if I had been as indolent as you?"

"I am sure I am willing to do whatever you require, Uncle Thomas. Have you any instructions?"

"Well, not just now, except to let me know all you can learn about the newsboy. Has he any other source of income except selling papers?"

"I believe he does a few odd jobs now and then, but I don't suppose he earns much outside."

"I was talking with him this morning."

"You were!" ejaculated Stephen in a tone of curiosity. "Did you tell him you felt an interest in him?"

"No, and I don't want you to tell him so. I suggested that he could make a better income by leaving Chicago, and going farther West."

"I think I might like to do that, Uncle Thomas."

"Then why don't you?"

"I can't go without money."

"You could take up a quarter-section of land, and start in as a farmer. I could give you a lift that way if I thought you were in earnest."

"I don't think I should succeed as a farmer," said Stephen, with a grimace.

"Too hard work, eh?"

"I am willing to work hard, but that isn't in my line."

"Well, let that go. You asked if I had any instructions. Find opportunities of talking with the boy, and speak in favor of going West."

"I will. Is there anything more?"

"No, I believe not."

"You couldn't let me have a couple of dollars extra, could you, uncle?"

" Why should I? "

" I—I felt sick last week, and had to call in a doctor, and then get some medicine."

" There's one dollar! Don't ask me for any more extras."

" He's awfully close-fisted," grumbled Stephen. " I am glad he didn't ask me the doctor's name, or what my sickness was. It might have bothered me a little to tell."

" I am afraid King might visit Chicago, and find out the boy," said Browning to himself as he continued his walk. " That would never do, for he is a sharp fellow, and would put the boy on my track if he saw any money in it. My best course is to get this Luke out of Chicago, if I can."

Stephen Webb made it in his way to fall in with Luke when he was selling afternoon papers.

" This is rather a slow way of making a fortune, isn't it, Luke? " he asked.

" Yes; I have no thoughts of making a fortune at the newspaper business."

" Do you always expect to remain in it?" continued Webb.

" Well, no," answered Luke, with a smile. " If I live to be fifty or sixty I think I should find it rather tiresome."

" You are right there."

" But I don't see any way of getting out of it just yet. There may be an opening for me by and by."

" The chances for a young fellow in Chicago are

not very good.   Here aι,ι I—twenty-five years old
—and with no prospects to speak of."

" A good many people seem to make good livings,
and many grow rich, in Chicago."

" Yes, if you've got money you can make money.
Did you ever think of going West? "

Luke looked a little surprised.

" A gentleman was speaking to me on that subject this morning," he said.

" What did he say to you? " asked Stephen, curiously.

" He recommended me to go West, but did not
seem to approve of California."

" Why not?   Had he ever been there? "

" He said he had visited San Francisco, but had
never been in the interior."

" What a whopper that was! " thought Stephen
Webb.   " Why should Uncle Thomas say that? "

" What sort of a looking man was he?   Had you
ever seen him before? " he inquired.

" He is a peculiar-looking man—has a wart on his
right cheek."

" Did he mention the particular part of the
West? "

" No; he said he would look out for a chance for
me."

" It is curious Uncle Thomas feels such an interest in that boy," Webb said to himself, meditatively.
" There's some reason.   ¨ wish I could find out."

CHAPTER XXIV

MRS. MERTON PASSES A PLEASANT EVENING

Ambrose Kean called with Luke an evening or two later to thank Mrs. Merton in person for her kindness. They arrived ten minutes after Mrs. Tracy and Harold had started for Hooley's Theater, and thus were saved an embarrassing meeting with two persons who would have treated them frigidly.

They were conducted upstairs by the servant, and were ushered into Mrs. Merton's room.

Ambrose Kean was naturally ill at ease, knowing that Mrs. Merton was acquainted with the error he had committed. But the old lady received him cordially.

"I am glad to meet the son of my old schoolmate, Mary Robinson," she said.

"In spite of his unworthiness?" returned Ambrose, his cheek flushing with shame.

"I don't know whether he is unworthy. That remains to be seen."

"You know I yielded to temptation and committed a theft."

"Yes; but it was to help your mother."

"It was, but that does not relieve me from guilt.'

151

"You are right; still, it greatly mitigates it. Take my advice; forget it, and never again yield to a similar temptation."

"I will not, indeed, Mrs. Merton," said the young man, earnestly. "I feel that I have been very fortunate in escaping the consequences of my folly, and in enlisting your sympathy."

"That is well! Let us forget this disagreeable circumstance, and look forward to the future. How is Mary—your mother?"

"She is an invalid."

"And poor. There is a remedy for poverty. Let us also hope there is a remedy for her ill-health. But tell me, why did you not come to see me before? You have been some time in Chicago."

"True, but I knew you were a rich lady. I didn't think you would remember or care to hear from one so poor and obscure as my mother."

"Come, I consider that far from a compliment," said the old lady. "You really thought as badly of me as that?"

"I know you better now," said Ambrose, gratefully.

"It is well you do. You have no idea how intimate your mother and I used to be. She is five years my junior, I think, so that I regarded her as a younger sister. It is many years since we met. And how is she looking?"

"She shows the effects of bad health, but I don't think she looks older than her years."

"We have both changed greatly, no doubt. It is to be expected. But you can tell her that I have not forgotten the favorite companion of my school days."

"I will do so, for I know it will warm her heart and brighten her up."

"When we were girls together our worldly circumstances did not greatly differ. But I married, and my husband was very successful in business."

"While she married and lost all she had."

"It is often so. It might have been the other way. Your mother might have been rich, and I poor; but I don't think she would have been spoiled by prosperity any more than I have been. Now tell me how you are situated."

"I am a clerk, earning twelve dollars a week."

"And your employer—is he kind and considerate?"

"He is just, but he has strict notions. Had he learned my slip the other day he would have discharged me, perhaps had me arrested. Now, thanks to your prompt kindness, he knows and will know nothing of it."

"Is he likely to increase your salary?"

"He will probably raise me to fifteen dollars a week next January. Then I can get along very well. At present it is difficult for me, after sending my mother four dollars a week, to live on the balance of my salary."

"I should think it would be."

"Still, I would have made it do, but for mother's falling sick, and so needing a larger allowance."

"I hope she is not seriously ill," said Mrs. Merton, with solicitude.

"No, fortunately not. I think she will be as well as usual in a few weeks."

"Tell her I inquired particularly for her, and that I send her my love and remembrance."

"I shall be only too glad to do so."

It might not prove interesting to the reader to detail all the conversation that followed. The old lady asked many questions, and furnished some reminiscences of her early days. The time slipped away so rapidly that Luke was surprised when, looking at the French clock on the mantel, he saw that it lacked but a quarter of ten o'clock.

"Mr. Kean," he said, glancing at the clock, "it is getting late."

"So it is," said Ambrose, rising. "I am afraid we have been trespassing upon your kindness, Mrs. Merton."

"Not at all!" said Mrs. Merton, promptly. "I have enjoyed the evening, I can assure you. Mr. Kean, you must call again."

"I shall be glad to do so, if you will permit me."

"I wish you to do so. Luke will come with you. I shall want to hear more of your mother, and how she gets along."

As they were leaving, Mrs. Merton slipped into the hand of Ambrose Kean an envelope.

" The contents is for your mother," she said. " I have made the check payable to you."

" Thank you. It is another mark of your kindness."

When Ambrose Kean examined the check, he ascertained to his joy that it was for a hundred dollars.

" What a splendid old lady she is, Luke ! " he said, enthusiastically.

" She is always kind, Mr. Kean. I have much to be grateful to her for. I wish I could say the same of other members of the family."

" What other members of the family are there? "

" A niece, Mrs. Tracy, and her son, Harold."

" Why didn't we see them to-night? "

" I don't know. I suppose they were out."

The next day Ambrose handed the check to his employer and asked if he would indorse it, and so enable him to draw the money.

James Cooper took the check and examined the signature.

" Eliza Merton," said he. " Is it the rich Mrs. Merton who lives on Prairie Avenue? "

" Yes, sir."

" Indeed; I did not know that you were acquainted with her."

" She and my mother were schoolmates."

" And so you keep up the acquaintance? "

" I spent last evening at her house. This check is a gift from her to my mother."

Ambrose Kean rose greatly in the estimation or
his employer when the latter learned that Kean had
such an aristocratic friend, and he was treated with
more respect and consideration than before. It need
not excite surprise, for it is the way of the world.

Meanwhile Harold and his mother had enjoyed
themselves at the theater.

" I suppose Aunt Eliza wet to bed early,
Harold," said Mrs. Tracy, as they were on their
way home.

" Went to roost with the hens," suggested Harold,
laughing at what he thought to be a good joke.

" Probably it is as well for her," said his mother.
" It isn't good for old people to sit up late."

It was about half-past eleven when they were admitted by the drowsy servant.

" I suppose Mrs. Merton went to bed long ago,
Laura," said Mrs. Tracy.

" No, ma'am, she set up later than usual."

" That is odd. I thought she would feel lonely."

" Oh, she had company, ma'am."

" Company ! Who? "

" Master Luke was here all the evenin', and a
young man with him."

Mrs. Tracy frowned ominously.

" The sly young artful ! " she said to Harold when
they were alone. " He is trying all he can to get or
aunt's weak side. Something will have to be done
or we shall be left out in the cold."

CHAPTER XXV

MRS. TRACY'S BROTHER

A day or two later, while Mrs. Merton was in the city shopping, accompanied by Luke, a man of thirty years of age ascended the steps of the house on Prairie Avenue and rang the bell.

"Is Mrs. Tracy at home?" he asked of the servant who answered the bell.

"Yes, sir; what name shall I give?"

"Never mind about the name. Say it is an old friend."

"Won't you come in, sir?"

"Yes, I believe I will."

Mrs. Tracy received the message with surprise mingled with curiosity.

"Who can it be?" she asked herself.

She came downstairs without delay.

The stranger, who had taken a seat in the hall, rose and faced her.

"Don't you know me, Louisa?" he asked.

"Is it you, Warner?" she exclaimed, surprised and startled.

"Yes," he answered, laughing. "It's a good while since we met."

157

" Five years. And have you——"

" What—reformed? "

" Yes."

" Well, I can't say as to that. I can only tell you that I am not wanted by the police at present. Is the old lady still alive? "

" Aunt Eliza? "

" Of course."

" Yes, she is alive and well."

" I thought perhaps she might have died, and left you in possession of her property."

" Not yet. I don't think she has any intention of dying for a considerable number of years."

" That is awkward. Has she done nothing for you? "

" We have a free home here, and she makes me a moderate allowance, but she is not disposed to part with much of her money while she lives."

" I am sorry for that. I thought you might be able to help me to some money. I am terribly hard up."

" You always were, no matter how much money you had."

" I never had much. The next thing is, how does the old lady feel towards me? "

" I don't think she feels very friendly, though nothing has passed between us respecting you for a long time. She has very strict notions about honesty, and when you embezzled your employer's money you got into her black books."

"That was a youthful indiscretion," said Warner, smiling. "Can't you convince her of that?"

"I doubt if I can lead her to think of it in that light."

"I know what that means, Louisa. You want to get the whole of the old lady's property for yourself and that boy of yours. You always were selfish."

"No, Warner, though I think I am entitled to the larger part of aunt's money, I don't care to have you left out in the cold. I will do what I can to reconcile her to you."

"Come, that's fair and square. You're a trump, Louisa. You have not forgotten that I am your brother."

"No, I am not so selfish as you think. If I don't succeed in restoring you to Aunt Eliza's good graces, and she chooses to leave me all her property, I promise to take care of you and allow you a fair income."

"That's all right, but I would rather the old lady would provide for me herself."

"Do you doubt my word?"

"No, but your idea of what would be a fair income might differ from mine. How much do you think the old lady's worth?"

"Quarter of a million, I should think," replied Mrs. Tracy, guardedly.

"Yes, and considerably more, too."

"Perhaps so. I have no means of judging."

" Supposing it to be the figure you name, how much would you be willing to give me, if she leaves me out in the cold? "

" I am not prepared to say, Warner. I would see that you had no good reason to complain."

" I should prefer to have you name a figure, so that I might know what to depend upon."

But this Mrs. Tracy declined to do, though her brother continued to urge her.

" Where have you been for a few years past, Warner? " she asked.

" Floating about. At first I didn't dare to come back. It was a year at least before I heard that aunt had paid up the sum I got away with. When I did hear it I was in Australia."

" What did you do there? "

" I was a bookkeeper in Melbourne for a time. Then I went into the country. From Australia I came to California, and went to the mines. In fact, I have only just come from there."

" Didn't you manage to make money anywhere? "

" Yes, but it didn't stick by me. How much money do you think I have about me now? "

" I can't guess," said Mrs. Tracy, uneasily.

" Five dollars and a few cents. However, I am sure you will help me," he continued.

" Really, Warner, you mustn't hope for too much from me. I have but a small allowance from Aunt Eliza—hardly enough to buy necessary articles for Harold and myself."

" Then you can speak to aunt in my behalf."

" Yes, I can do that."

" Where is she?"

" She has gone out shopping this morning."

" Alone, or is Harold with her?"

" Neither," answered Mrs. Tracy, her brow darkening. " She has picked up a boy from the street, and installed him as a first favorite."

" That's queer, isn't it?"

" Yes; but Aunt Eliza was always queer."

" What's the boy's name?"

" Luke Walton."

" What's his character?"

" Sly—artful. He is scheming to have aunt leave him something in her will."

" If she leaves him a few hundred dollars it won't hurt us much."

" You don't know the boy. He won't be satisfied with that."

" You don't mean to say that his influence over aunt is dangerous?"

" Yes, I do."

" Can't you get her to bounce him?"

" I have done what I could, but she seems to be infatuated. If he were a gentleman's son I shouldn't mind so much, but Harold saw him the other day selling papers near the Sherman House."

" Do you think aunt's mind is failing?"

" She seems rational enough on all other subjects. She was always shrewd and sharp, you know."

" Well, that's rather an interesting state or things. I haven't returned to Chicago any too soon."

" Why do you say that?"

" Because it will be my duty to spoil the chances of this presuming young man."

" That is easier said than done. You forget that Aunt Eliza thinks a great deal more of him than she does of you."

" I haven't a doubt that you are right."

" Then what can you do?"

" Convince her that he is a scapegrace. Get him into a scrape, in other words."

" But he is too smart to be dishonest, if that is what you mean."

" It is not necessary for him to be dishonest. It is only necessary for her to think he is dishonest."

There was some further conversation. As Warner Powell was leaving the house, after promising to call in the evening, he met on the steps Mrs. Merton, under the escort of Luke Walton.

The old lady eyed him sharply.

CHAPTER XXVI

THE PRODIGAL'S RECEPTION

"Don't you know me, Aunt Eliza?" asked Warner Powell, casting down his eyes under the sharp glance of the old lady.

"So it is you, is it?" responded Mrs. Merton, in a tone which could not be considered cordial.

"Yes, it is I. I hope you are not sorry to see me?"

"Humph! It depends on whether you have improved or not."

Luke Walton listened with natural interest and curiosity. This did not suit Mrs. Tracy, who did not care to have a stranger made acquainted with her brother's peccadilloes.

"Warner," she said, "I think Aunt Eliza will do you the justice to listen to your explanation. I imagine, young man, Mrs. Merton will not require your services any longer to-day."

The last words were addressed to Luke.

"Yes, Luke; you can go," said the old lady, in a very different tone.

Luke bowed, and left the house.

"Louisa," said Mrs. Merton, "in five minutes you may bring your brother up to my room."

"Thank you, aunt."

When they entered the apartment they found the old lady seated in a rocking-chair awaiting them.

"So you have reformed, have you?" she asked, abruptly.

"I hope so, Aunt Eliza."

"I hope so, too. It is full time. Where have you been?"

"To Australia, California, and elsewhere."

"A rolling stone gathers no moss."

"In this case it applies," said Warner. "I have earned more or less money, but I have none now."

"How old are you?"

"Thirty."

"A young man ought not to be penniless at that age. If you had remained in your place at Mr. Afton's, and behaved yourself, you would be able to tell a different story."

"I know it, aunt."

"Don't be too hard upon him, Aunt Eliza," put in Mrs. Tracy. "He is trying to do well now."

"I am very glad to hear it."

"Would you mind my inviting him to stay here for a time? The house is large, you know."

Mrs. Merton paused. She didn't like the arrangement, but she was a just and merciful woman, and it was possible that Warner had reformed, though she was not fully satisfied on that point.

"For a time," she answered, "till he can find employment."

"Thank you, Aunt Eliza," said the young man, relieved, for he had been uncertain how his aunt would treat him. "I hope to show that your kindness is appreciated."

"I am rather tired now," responded Mrs. Merton, as an indication that the interview was over.

"We'd better go and let aunt rest," said Warner, with alacrity. He did not feel altogether comfortable in the society of the old lady.

When they were alone Mrs. Tracy turned to her brother with a smile of satisfaction.

"You have reason to congratulate yourself on your reception," she said.

"I don't know about that. The old woman wasn't very complimentary."

"Be careful how you speak of her. She might hear you, or the servants might, and report."

"Well, she is an old woman, isn't she?"

"It is much better to refer to her as the old lady —better still to speak of her as Aunt Eliza."

"I hope she will make up her mind to do something for me."

"She has; she gives you a home in this house."

"I would a good deal rather have her pay my board outside, where I would feel more independent."

"I have been thinking, Warner, you might become her secretary and man of business. In that case she would dispense with this boy, whose presence bodes danger to us all."

" I wouldn't mind being her man of business, to take charge of her money, but as to trotting round town with her like a lame poodle, please excuse me."

" Warner," said his sister, rather sharply, " just remember, if you please, that beggars can't be choosers."

" Perhaps not, but this plan of yours would be foolish. She wouldn't like it, nor would I. Why don't you put Harold up to offering his services? He's as large as this boy, isn't he? "

" He is about the same size."

" Then it would be a capital plan. You would get rid of the boy that way."

" You forget that Harold has not finished his education. He is now attending a commercial school. I should like to have him go to college, but he doesn't seem to care about it."

" So, after all, the boy seems to be a necessity."

" I would prefer a different boy, less artful and designing."

" How much does the old woman—beg pardon, the old lady—pay him? "

" I don't know. Harold asked Luke, but he wouldn't tell. I have no doubt he manages to secure twice as much as his services are worth. He's got on Aunt Eliza's blind side."

" Just what I would like to do, but I have never been able to discover that she had any."

" Did you take notice of the boy? "

"Yes; he's rather a good-looking youngster, it seems to me."

"How can you say so?" demanded Mrs. Tracy, sharply. "There's a very common look about him, I think. He isn't nearly as good-looking as Harold."

"Harold used to look like you," said Warner, with a smile. "Natural you should think him good-looking. But don't it show a little self-conceit, Louisa?"

"That's a poor joke," answered his sister, coldly. "What are you going to do?"

"Going out to see if I can find any of my old acquaintances."

"You had much better look for a position, as Aunt Eliza hinted."

"Don't be in such a hurry, Louisa. Please bear in mind that I have only just arrived in Chicago after an absence of five years."

"Dinner will be ready in half an hour."

"Thank you. I don't think I should like a second interview with Aunt Eliza quite so soon. I will lunch outside."

"A lunch outside costs money, and you are not very well provided in that way."

"Don't trouble yourself about that, Louisa. I intend to be very economical.

"My estimable sister is about as mean as anyone I know," said Warner to himself as he left the house. "Between her and the old woman, I don't

think I shall find it very agreeable living here. A
cheap boarding house would be infinitely prefer-
able."

On State Street Warner Powell fell in with Stephen Webb, an old acquaintance.

"Is it you, Warner?" asked Webb, in surprise.
"It's an age since I saw you."

"So it is. I haven't been in Chicago for five
years."

"I remember. A little trouble, wasn't there?"

"Yes; but I'm all right now, except that I haven't
any money to speak of."

"That's my situation exactly."

"However, I've got an old aunt worth a million,
more or less, only she doesn't fully appreciate her
nephew."

"And I have an uncle, pretty well to do, who isn't
so deeply impressed with my merits as I wish he
were."

"I am staying with my aunt just at present, but
hope to have independent quarters soon. One
trouble is, she takes a fancy to a boy named Luke
Walton."

"Luke Walton!" repeated Stephen, in amazement.

"Do you know him?"

"Yes, my uncle has set me to spy on him—why,
I haven't been able to find out. So he is in favor
with your aunt?"

"Yes, he calls at the house every day, and is in

her employ. Sometimes she goes out shopping with him."

" That's strange. Let us drop into the Saratoga and compare notes."

They turned into Dearborn Street, and sat down to lunch in the Saratoga, a popular restaurant already referred to.

CHAPTER XXVII

UNCLE AND NEPHEW

" So this boy is an object of interest to your uncle? " resumed Warner Powell.

" Yes."

" Does he give any reason for his interest? "

" No, except that he is inclined to help him when there is an opportunity."

" Does the boy know him? "

" No."

" Has he met your uncle? "

" Yes; Uncle Thomas frequently visits Chicago —he lives in Milwaukee—and stays at the Sherman when he is here. He has stopped and bought a paper of Luke once or twice."

" I remember my sister told me this boy Luke was a newsboy."

" How did he get in with your aunt? "

" I don't know. I presume it was a chance acquaintance. However that may be, the young rascal seems to have got on her blind side, and to be installed first favorite."

" Your sister doesn't like it? "

" Not much. Between you and me, Louisa ·

Mrs. Tracy—means to inherit all the old lady's property, and doesn't like to have anyone come in, even for a trifle. She'll have me left out in the cold if she can, but I mean to have something to say to that. In such matters you can't trust even your own sister."

"I agree with you, Warner."

The two young men ate a hearty dinner, and then adjourned to a billiard room, where they spent the afternoon over the game. Warner reached home in time for supper.

"Where have you been, Warner?" asked Mrs. Tracy.

"Looking for work," was the answer.

"What success did you meet with?"

"Not much as yet. I fell in with an old acquaintance, who may assist me in that direction."

"I am glad you have lost no time in seeking employment. It will please aunt."

Warner Powell suppressed a smile. He wondered what Mrs. Merton would have thought could she have seen in what manner he prosecuted his search for employment.

"This is Harold," said Mrs. Tracy, proudly, as her son came in. "Harold, this is your Uncle Warner."

Harold shrugged his shoulders. He did not seem particularly glad to meet his new relative. He scanned him critically from head to foot, and inwardly pronounced him very ill dressed.

"So you are Harold," said his uncle. "I re-member you in short pants. You have changed considerably in five years."

"Yes, I suppose so," answered Harold, curtly. "Where have you been?"

"In Australia, California, and so on."

"How long are you going to stay in Chicago?"

"That depends on whether I can find employment. If you hear of a place let me know."

"I don't know of any unless Aunt Eliza will take you into her employ in place of that newsboy, Luke Walton."

"She can have me if she will pay me enough salary. How much does Luke get?"

"I don't know. He won't tell."

"Do you like him?"

"I don't consider him a fit associate for me. He is a common newsboy."

"Does Aunt Eliza know that?"

"Yes; it makes no difference to her. She's in-fatuated with him."

"I wish she were infatuated with me. I shall have to ask Luke his secret. Aunt Eliza doesn't prefer him to you, does she?"

"I have no doubt she does. She's very queer about some things."

"Harold," said his mother, solicitously, "I don't think you pay Aunt Eliza enough attention. Old persons, you know, like to receive courtesies."

"I treat her politely, don't I?" asked Harold,

aggressively. "I can't be dancing attendance upon her and flattering her all the time."

"From what I have seen of Luke Walton," thought Warner Powell, "I should decidedly prefer him to this nephew of mine. He seems conceited and disagreeable. Of course, it won't do to tell Louisa that, for she evidently admires her graceless cub, because he is hers."

"Are you intimate with this Luke?" asked Warner, mischievously.

"What do you take me for?" demanded Harold, offended. "I am not in the habit of getting intimate with street boys."

Warner Powell laughed.

"I am not so proud as you, Nephew Harold," he said. "Travelers pick up strange companions. In San Francisco I became intimate with a Chinaman."

"You don't mean it?" exclaimed Harold, in incredulity and disgust.

"Yes, I do."

"You weren't in the laundry business with him, were you?" went on Harold, with a sneer.

"I should like to give my nephew a good shaking," thought Warner. "He knows how to be impertinent.

"No," he answered aloud. "The laundry business may be a very good one—I should like the income it produces even now—but I don't think I have the necessary talent for it. My Chinese friend was

a commission merchant worth at least a hundred
thousand dollars. I wasn't above borrowing money
from him sometimes."

"Of course, that makes a difference," said Mrs.
Tracy, desiring to make peace between her brother
and son. "He must have been a superior man.
Harold thought you meant a common Chinaman,
such as we have in Chicago."

The reunited family sat down to supper together.
Warner Powell tried to make himself agreeable, and
succeeded in thawing his aunt's coldness. He appeared to advantage compared with Harold, whose
disposition was not calculated to win friends for
himself.

After supper Warner made an excuse for going
out.

"I have an engagement with a friend who knows
of a position he thinks I can secure," he said.

"I hope you won't be late," said Mrs. Tracy.

"No, I presume not, but you had better give me
a pass key."

Mrs. Tracy did so reluctantly. She was afraid
Harold might want to join his uncle; but the
nephew was not taken with his new relative, and
made no such proposal.

In reality, Warner Powell had made an engagement to go to McVicker's Theater with his friend
Stephen Webb, who had arranged to meet him at
the Sherman House.

While waiting, Warner, who had an excellent

memory for faces, recognized Luke, who was
selling papers at his usual post. There was some
startling news in the evening papers—a collision
on Lake Michigan—and Luke had ordered an unusual supply, which occupied him later than his
ordinary hour. He had taken a hasty supper at
Brockway & Milan's, foreseeing that he would not
be home till late.

"Aunt Eliza's boy!" thought Warner. "I may
as well take this opportunity to cultivate his acquaintance."

He went up to Luke and asked for a paper.

"You don't remember me?" he said, with a smile.

"No," answered Luke, looking puzzled.

"I saw you on Prairie Avenue this morning.
Mrs. Merton is my aunt."

"I remember you now. Are you Mrs. Tracy's
brother?"

"Yes, and the uncle of Harold. How do you and
Harold get along?"

"Not at all. He takes very little notice of me."

"He is a snob. Being his uncle, I take the liberty
to say it."

Luke smiled.

"There is no love lost between us," he said. "I
would like to be more friendly, but he treats me
like an enemy."

"He is jealous of your favor with my aunt."

"There is no occasion for it. He is a relative, and
I am only in her employ."

" She thinks a good deal of you, doesn't she? "

" She treats me very kindly."

" Harold suggested to me this evening at supper
that I should take your place. You needn't feel
anxious. I have no idea of doing so, and she
wouldn't have me if I had."

" I think a man like you could do better."

" I am willing to. But here comes my friend,
who is going to the theater with me."

Looking up, Luke was surprised to see Stephen
Webb.

CHAPTER XXVIII

HAROLD'S TEMPTATION

Mrs. Merton was rather astonished when her grandnephew Harold walked into her room one day and inquired for her health. (She had been absent from the dinner table on account of a headache.)

"Thank you, Harold," she said. "I am feeling a little better."

"Have you any errand you would like to have me do for you?"

Mrs. Merton was still more surprised, for offers of services were rare with Harold.

"Thank you again," she said, "but Luke was here this morning, and I gave him two or three commissions."

Harold frowned a little at the mention of Luke's name, but he quickly smoothed his brow, for he wished to propitiate his aunt.

"Perhaps you would like me to read to you, Aunt Eliza."

"Thank you, but I am a little afraid it wouldn't be a good thing for my head. How are you getting on at school, Harold?"

"Pretty well."

"You don't want to go to college?"

"No. I think I would rather be a business man."

"Well, you know your own tastes best."

"Aunt Eliza," said Harold, after a pause, "I want to ask a favor of you."

"Speak out, Harold."

"Won't you be kind enough to give me ten dollars?"

"Ten dollars," repeated the old lady, eying Harold closely. "Why do you want ten dollars?"

"You see, mother keeps me very close. All the fellows have more money to spend than I."

"How much does your mother give you as an allowance?"

"Two dollars a week."

"It seems to me that is liberal, considering that you don't have to pay for your board or clothes."

"A boy in my position is expected to spend money."

"Who expects it?"

"Why, everybody."

"By the way, what is your position?" asked the old lady, pointedly.

"Why," said Harold, uneasily, "I am supposed to be rich, as I live in a nice neighborhood on a fashionable street."

"That doesn't make you rich, does it?"

"No," answered Harold, with hesitation.

"You don't feel absolutely obliged to spend more than your allowance, do you?"

"Well, you see, the fellows think I am mean if I don't. There's Ben Clark has an allowance of five dollars a week, and he is three months younger than I am."

"Then I think his parents or guardians are very unwise. How does he spend his liberal allowance?"

"Oh, he has a good time."

"I am afraid it isn't the sort of good time I would approve."

"Luke has more money than I have, and he is only a newsboy," grumbled Harold.

"How do you know?"

"I notice he always has money."

"I doubt whether he spends half a dollar a week on his own amusement. He has a mother and young brother to support."

"He says so!"

"So you doubt it?"

"It may be true."

"If you find it isn't true you can let me know."

Harold did not answer. He had no real doubt on the subject, but liked to say something ill-natured about Luke.

"I am sorry that you think so much more of Luke than of me," complained Harold.

"How do you know I do?"

"Mother thinks so as well as I."

"Suppose we leave Luke out of consideration. I shall think as much of you as you deserve."

Harold rose from his seat.

"As you have no errand for me, Aunt Eliza, I will go," he said.

"Wait a moment."

Mrs. Merton unlocked a drawer in a work table, took out a morocco pocketbook, and extracted therefrom a ten-dollar bill.

"You have asked me a favor, and I will grant it—for once," she said. "Here are ten dollars."

"Thank you," said Harold, joyfully.

"I won't even ask how you propose to spend it. I thought of doing so, but it would imply distrust, and for this occasion I won't show any."

"You are very kind, Aunt Eliza."

"I am glad you think so. You are welcome to the money."

Harold left the room in high spirits. He decided not to let his mother know that he had received so large a sum, as she might inquire to what use he intended to put it; and some of his expenditures, he felt pretty sure, would not be approved by her.

He left the house, and going downtown, joined a couple of friends of his own stamp. They adjourned to a billiard saloon, and between billiards, bets upon the game, and drinks, Harold managed to spend three dollars before suppertime.

Three days later the entire sum given him by his aunt was gone.

When Harold made the discovery, he sighed. His dream was over. It had been pleasant as long as it lasted, but it was over too soon.

"Now I must go back to my mean allowance," he said to himself, in a discontented tone. "Aunt Eliza might give me ten dollars every week just as well as not. She is positively rolling in wealth, while I have to grub along like a newsboy. Why, that fellow Luke has a great deal more money than I."

A little conversation which he had with his Uncle Warner made his discontent more intense.

"Hello, Harold, what makes you look so blue?" he asked one day.

"Because I haven't got any money," answered Harold.

"Doesn't your mother or Aunt Eliza give you any?"

"I get a little, but it isn't as much as the other fellows get."

"How much?"

"Two dollars a week."

"It is more than I had when I was of your age."

"That doesn't make it any better."

"Aunt Eliza isn't exactly lavish; still, she pays Luke Walton generously."

"Do you know how much he gets a week?" asked Harold, eagerly.

"Ten dollars."

"Ten dollars!" ejaculated Harold. "You don't really mean it."

"Yes, I do. I saw her pay him that sum yesterday. I asked her if it wasn't liberal. She admitted it, but said he had a mother and brother to support!"

"It's a shame!" cried Harold, passionately.

"Why is it? The money is her own, isn't it?"

"She ought not to treat a stranger better than her own nephew."

"That means me, I judge," said Warner, smiling. "Well, there isn't anything we can do about it, is there?"

"No, I don't know as there is," replied Harold, slowly.

But he thought over what his uncle had told him, and it made him very bitter. He brooded over it till it seemed to him as if it were a great outrage. He felt that he was treated with the greatest injustice. He was incensed with his aunt, but still more so with Luke Walton, whom he looked upon as an artful adventurer.

It was while he was cherishing these feelings that a great temptation came to him. He found, one day in the street, a bunch of keys of various sizes attached to a small steel ring. He picked it up, and quick as a flash there came to him the thought of the drawer in his aunt's work table, from which he had seen her take out the morocco pocketbook. He had observed that the ten-dollar bill she gave him was only one out of a large roll, and his cupidity was aroused. He rapidly concocted a scheme by which he would be enabled to provide himself with money, and throw suspicion upon Luke.

CHAPTER XXIX

HAROLD'S THEFT

The next morning, Mrs. Merton, escorted by Luke, went to make some purchases in the city. Mrs. Tracy went out, also, having an engagement with one of her friends living on Cottage Grove Avenue. Harold went out directly after breakfast, but returned at half-past ten. He went upstairs and satisfied himself that, except the servants, he was alone in the house.

"The coast is clear," he said, joyfully. "Now, if the key only fits."

He went to his aunt's sitting room, and, not anticipating any interruption, directed his steps at once to the small table, from a drawer in which he had seen Mrs. Merton take the morocco pocketbook. He tried one key after another, and finally succeeded in opening the drawer. He drew it out with nervous anxiety, fearing that the pocketbook might have been removed, in which case all his work would have been thrown away.

But no! Fortune favored him this time, if it can be called a favor. There, in plain sight, was the morocco pocketbook. Harold, pale with excitement, seized and opened it. His eyes glistened as he saw that it was well filled. He took out the roll of bills, and counted them. There were five ten-dollar bills and three fives—sixty-five dollars in all. There would have been more, but Mrs. Merton, before going out, had taken four fives, which she intended to use.

It was Harold's first theft, and he trembled with agitation as he thrust the pocketbook into his pocket. He would have trembled still more if he had known that his mother's confidential maid and seamstress, Felicie Lacouvreur, had seen everything through the crevice formed by the half-open door.

Felicie smiled to herself as she moved noiselessly away from her post of concealment.

"Master Harold is trying a dangerous experiment," she said to herself. "Now he is in my power. He has been insolent to me more than once, as if, forsooth, he were made of superior clay, but Felicie, though only a poor servant, is not, thank Heaven, a thief, as he is. It is a very interesting drama. I shall wait patiently till it is quite played out."

In his hurry, Harold came near leaving the room with the table drawer open. But he bethought himself in time, went back, and locked it securely. It was like shutting the stable door after the horse was stolen. Then, with the stolen money in his possession, he left the house. He did not wish to be found at home when his aunt returned.

Harold had sixty-five dollars in his pocket—an amount quite beyond what he had ever before had at his disposal—but it must be admitted that he did not feel as happy as he had expected. If he had come by it honestly; if, for instance, it had been given him, his heart would have beat high with exultation, but as it was, he walked along with clouded brow. Presently he ran across one of his friends, who noticed his discomposure.

"What's the matter, Harold?" he asked. "You are in the dumps."

"Oh, no," answered Harold, forcing himself to assume a more cheerful aspect. "I have no reason to feel blue."

"You are only acting, then? I must congratulate you on your success. You look for all the world like the knight of the sorrowful countenance."

"Who is he?" asked Harold, who was not literary.

"Don Quixote. Did you never hear of him?"

"No."

"Then your education has been neglected. What are you going to do to-day?"

"I don't know."

"Suppose we visit a dime museum?"

"All right."

"That is, if you have any money. I am high and dry."

"Yes, I have some money."

They went to a dime museum on Clark Street.
Harold surprised his companion by paying for the
two tickets out of a five-dollar bill.

" You're flush, Harold," said his friend. " Has
anybody left you a fortune? "

" No," answered Harold, uneasily. " I've been
saving up money lately."

" You have? Why, I've heard of your being at
theaters, playing billiards, and so on."

" Look here, Robert Greve, I don't see why you
need trouble yourself so much about where I get
my money."

" Don't be cranky, Harold," said Robert, good-
humoredly, " I won't say another word. Only I
am glad to find my friends in a healthy financial
condition. I only wish I could say the same of
myself."

There happened to be a matinée at the Grand
Opera House, and Harold proposed going. First,
however, they took a nice lunch at Brockway &
Milan's, a mammoth restaurant on Clark Street,
Harold paying the bill.

As they came out of the theater, Luke Walton
chanced to pass.

" Good-afternoon, Harold," he said.

Harold tossed his head, but did not reply.

" Who is that boy—one of your acquaintances?"
asked Robert Greve.

" He works for my aunt," answered Harold. " It
is like his impudence to speak to me."

"Why shouldn't he speak to you, if you know him?" said Robert Greve, who did not share Harold's foolish pride.

"He appears to think he is my equal," continued Harold.

"He seems a nice boy."

"You don't know him as I do. He is a common newsboy."

"Suppose he is; that doesn't hurt him, does it?"

"You don't know what I mean. You don't think a common newsboy fit to associate with on equal terms, do you?"

Robert Greve laughed.

"You are too high-toned, Harold," he said. "If he is a nice boy, I don't care what sort of business a friend of mine follows."

"Well, I do," snapped Harold, "and so does my mother. I don't believe in being friends with the ragtag and bobtail of society."

Luke Walton did not allow his feelings to be hurt by the decided rebuff he had received from Harold.

"I owe it to myself to act like a gentleman," he reflected. "If Harold doesn't choose to be polite, it is his lookout, not mine. He looks down upon me because I am a working boy. I don't mean always to be a newsboy or an errand boy. I shall work my way upwards as fast as I can, and, in time, I may come to fill a good place in society."

It will be seen that Luke was ambitious. He

looked above and beyond the present, and determined to improve his social condition.

It was six o'clock when Harold ascended the steps of the mansion on Prairie Avenue. He had devoted the day to amusement, but had derived very little pleasure from the money he had expended. He had very little left of the five-dollar bill which he had first changed at the dime museum. It was not easy to say where his money had gone, but it had melted away, in one shape or another.

"I wonder whether Aunt Eliza has discovered her loss," thought Harold. "I hope I shan't show any signs of nervousness when I meet her. I don't see how she can possibly suspect me. If anything is said about the lost pocketbook, I will try to throw suspicion on Luke Walton."

Harold did not stop to think how mean this would be. Self-preservation, it has been said, is the first law of nature, and self-preservation required that he should avert suspicion from himself by any means in his power. He went into the house whistling, as if to show that his mind was quite free from care.

In the hall he met Felicie.

"What do you think has happened, Master Harold?" asked the French maid.

"I don't know, I'm sure."

"Your aunt has been robbed. Some money has been taken from her room."

CHAPTER XXX

LUKE WALTON IS SUSPECTED OF THEFT

Harold was prepared for the announcement, as he felt confident his aunt would soon discover her loss, but he felt a little nervous, nevertheless.

"You don't mean it!" he ejaculated, in well-counterfeited surprise.

"It's a fact."

"When did Aunt Eliza discover her loss, Felicie?"

"As soon as she got home. She went to her drawer to put back some money she had on hand, and found the pocketbook gone."

"Was there much money in it?"

"She doesn't say how much."

"Well," said Harold, thinking it time to carry on the programme he had determined upon, "I can't say I am surprised."

"You are not surprised!" repeated Felicie, slowly. "Why? Do you know anything about it?"

"Do I know anything about it?" said Harold, coloring. "What do you mean by that?"

"Because you say you are not surprised. I was

surprised, and so was the old lady and your
mother."

"You must be very stupid, not to understand
what I mean," said Harold, annoyed.

"Then I am very stupid, for I do not know at
all why you are not surprised."

"I mean that the boy Aunt Eliza employs—that
boy Luke—has taken the money."

"Oh, you think the boy, Luke, has taken the
money."

"Certainly! Why shouldn't he? He is a poor
newsboy. It would be a great temptation to him.
You know he is always shown into Aunt Eliza's
sitting room, and is often there alone."

"That is true."

"And, of course, nothing is more natural than
that he should take the money."

"But the drawer was locked."

"He had some keys in his pocket, very likely.
Most boys have keys."

"Oh, most boys have keys. Have you, perhaps,
keys, Master Harold?"

"It seems to me you are asking very foolish
questions, Felicie. I have the key of my trunk."

"But do newsboys have trunks? Why should
this boy, Luke, have keys? I do not see."

"Well, I'll go upstairs," said Harold, who was
getting tired of the interview, and rather uneasy at
Felicie's remarks and questions.

As Felicie had said, Mrs. Merton discovered her

loss almost as soon as she came home. She had used but a small part of the money she took with her, and, not caring to carry it about with her, opened the drawer to replace it in the pocket-book.

To her surprise the pocketbook had disappeared.

Now, the contents of the pocketbook, though a very respectable sum, were not sufficient to put Mrs. Merton to any inconvenience. Still, no one likes to lose money, especially if there is reason to believe that it has been stolen, and Mrs. Merton felt annoyed. She drew out the drawer to its full extent, and examined it carefully in every part, but there was no trace of the morocco pocketbook.

She locked the door and went downstairs to her niece.

"What's the matter, Aunt Eliza?" asked Mrs. Tracy, seeing, at a glance, from her aunt's expression, that something had happened.

"There is a thief in the house!" said the old lady, abruptly.

"What!"

"There is a thief in the house!"

"What makes you think so?"

"You remember my small work table?"

"Yes."

"I have been in the habit of keeping a supply of money in a pocketbook in one of the drawers. I just opened the drawer, and the money is gone!"

"Was there much money in the pocketbook?"

"I happen to know just how much. There were sixty-five dollars."

"And you can find nothing of the pocketbook?"

"No; that and the money are both gone."

"I am sorry for your loss, Aunt Eliza."

"I don't care for the money. I shall not miss it. I am amply provided with funds, thanks to Providence. But it is the mystery that puzzles me. Who can have robbed me?"

Mrs. Tracy nodded her head significantly.

"I don't think there need be any mystery about that," she said, pointedly.

"Why not?"

"I can guess who robbed you."

"Then I should be glad to have you enlighten me, for I am quite at a loss to fix upon the thief."

"It's that boy of yours. I haven't a doubt of it."

"You mean Luke Walton?"

"Yes, the newsboy, whom you have so imprudently trusted."

"What are your reasons for thinking he is a thief?" asked the old lady, calmly.

"He is often alone in the room where the work table stands, is he not?"

"Yes; he waits for me there."

"What could be easier than for him to open the drawer and abstract the pocketbook?"

"It would be possible, but he would have to unlock the drawer."

"Probably he took an impression of tne lock some day, and had a key made."

"You are giving him credit for an unusual amount of cunning."

"I always supposed he was sly."

"I am aware, Louisa, that you never liked the boy."

"I admit that. What has happened seems to show that I was right."

"Now you are jumping to conclusions. You decide, without any proof, or even investigation, that Luke took the money."

"I feel convinced of it."

"It appears to me that you are not treating the boy fairly."

"My instinct tells me that it is he who has robbed you."

"Instinct would have no weight in law."

"If he didn't take it, who did?" asked Mrs. Tracy, triumphantly.

"That question is not easy to answer, Louisa."

"I am glad you admit so much, Aunt Eliza."

"I admit nothing; but I will think over the matter carefully, and investigate."

"Do so, Aunt Eliza! In the end you will agree with me."

"In the meanwhile, Louisa, there is one thing I must insist upon."

"What is that?"

"That you leave the matter wholly in my hands."

"Certainly, if you wish it."

"There are some circumstances connected with the robbery which I have not mentioned."

"What are they?" asked Mrs. Tracy, her face expressing curiosity.

"I shall keep them to myself for the present."

Mrs. Tracy looked disappointed.

"If you mention them to me, I may think of something that would help you."

"If I need help in that way, I will come to you."

"Meanwhile, shall you continue to employ the boy?"

"Yes; why not?"

"He might steal something more."

"I will risk it."

Mrs. Merton returned to her room, and presently Harold entered his mother's presence.

"What is this I hear about Aunt Eliza having some money stolen?" he asked.

"It is true. She has lost sixty-five dollars."

"Felicie told me something about it—that it was taken out of her drawer."

Mrs. Tracy went into particulars, unconscious that her son was better informed than herself.

"Does aunt suspect anyone?" asked Harold, uneasily.

"She doesn't, but I do."

"Who is it?"

"That boy, Luke Walton."

"The very one I thought of," said Harold, eagerly. "Did you mention him to Aunt Eliza?"

"Yes; but she is so infatuated with him that she didn't take the suggestion kindly. She has promised to investigate, however, and meanwhile doesn't want us to interfere."

"Things are working round as I want them," thought Harold.

CHAPTER XXXI

WHO STOLE THE MONEY?

Did Mrs. Merton suspect anyone of the theft? This is the question which will naturally suggest itself to the reader.

No thought of the real thief entered her mind. Though she was fully sensible of Harold's faults, though she knew him to be selfish, bad-tempered, and envious, she did not suppose him capable of theft. The one who occurred to her as most likely to have robbed her was her recently returned nephew, Warner Powell, who had been compelled to leave Chicago years before on account of having yielded to a similar temptation. She knew that he was hard up for money, and it was possible that he had opened the table drawer and abstracted the pocketbook. As to Luke Walton, she was not at all affected by the insinuations of her niece. She knew that Mrs. Tracy and Harold had a prejudice against Luke, and that this would make them ready to believe anything against him.

She was curious, however, to hear what Warner had to say about the robbery. Would he, too, try to throw suspicion upon Luke in order to screen

himself, if he were the real thief? This remained
to be proved.

Warner Powell did not return to the house till
five o'clock in the afternoon. His sister and Harold hastened to inform him of what had happened,
and to communicate their conviction that Luke
was the thief. Warner said little, but his own suspicions were different. He went upstairs, and made
his aunt a call.

"Well, aunt," he said, "I hear you have been
robbed."

"Yes, Warner, I have lost some money," answered the old lady, composedly.

"Louisa told me."

"Yes; she suspects Luke of being the thief. Do
you agree with her?"

"No, I don't," answered Warner.

Mrs. Merton's face brightened, and she looked
kindly at Warner.

"Then you don't share Louisa's prejudice against
Luke?" she said.

"No; I like the boy. I would sooner suspect
myself of stealing the money, for, you know, Aunt
Eliza, that my record is not a good one, and I am
sure Luke is an honest boy."

Mrs. Merton's face fairly beamed with delight.
She understood very well the low and unworthy
motives which influenced her niece and Harold, and
it was a gratifying surprise to find that her nephew
was free from envy and jealousy.

" Warner," she said, " what you say does you credit. In this particular case I know that Luke is innocent."

" You don't know the real thief? " asked Warner.

" No; but my reason for knowing that Luke is innocent I will tell you. The money was safe in my drawer when I went out this morning. It was taken during my absence from the house. Luke was with me during this whole time. Of course, it is impossible that he should be the thief, therefore."

" I see. Did you tell Louisa this? "

" No; I am biding my time. Besides, I am more likely to find the real thief if it is supposed that Luke is under suspicion."

" Tell me, truly, Aunt Eliza, didn't you suspect me? "

" Since you ask me, Warner, I will tell you frankly that it occurred to me as possible that you might have yielded to temptation."

" It would have been a temptation, for I have but twenty-five cents in my pocket. But even if I had known where you kept your money (which I didn't), I would have risked applying to you for a loan, or gift, as it would have turned out to be, rather than fall back into my old disreputable ways."

" I am very much encouraged by what you say, Warner. Here are ten dollars. Use it judiciously;

try to obtain employment, and when it is gone, you
may let me know."

"Aunt Eliza, you are kinder to me than I deserve.
I will make a real effort to secure employment, and
will not abuse your confidence."

"Keep that promise, Warner, and I will be your
friend. One thing more: don't tell Louisa what has
passed between us. I can, at any time, clear Luke,
but for the present I will let her think I am uncertain on that point. I shall not forget that you took
the boy's part where your sister condemned him."

"Louisa and Harold can see no good in the boy;
but I have observed him carefully, and formed my
own opinion."

Warner could have done nothing better calculated
to win his aunt's favor than to express a favorable
opinion of Luke. It must be said, however, in justice to him, that this had not entered into his calcu-
lations. He really felt kindly towards the boy whom
his sister denounced as "sly and artful," and liked
him much better than his own nephew, Harold, who,
looking upon Warner as a poor relation, had not
thought it necessary to treat him with much respect
or attention. He had a better heart and a better
disposition than Mrs. Tracy or Harold, notwith-
standing his early shortcomings.

"Who could have been the thief?" Warner asked
himself, as he left his aunt's sitting room. "Could
it have been Harold?"

He resolved to watch his nephew carefully and

seek some clew that would lead to a solution of the mystery.

"I hope it isn't my nephew," he said to himself. "I don't want him to follow in the steps of his scapegrace uncle. But I would sooner suspect him than Luke Walton. They say blood is thicker than water, but I confess that I like the newsboy better than I do my high-toned nephew."

"Have you made any discovery of the theft, Aunt Eliza?" asked Mrs. Tracy, as her aunt seated herself at the evening repast.

"Nothing positive," answered the old lady, significantly.

"Have you discovered anything at all?"

"I have discovered who is not the thief," said Mrs. Merton.

"Then you had suspicions?"

"No definite suspicions."

"Wouldn't it be well to talk the matter freely over with me? Something might be suggested."

"I beg your pardon, Louisa, but I think it would be well to banish this disagreeable matter from our table talk. If I should stand in need of advice, I will consult you."

"I don't want to obtrude my advice, but I will venture to suggest that you call in a private detective."

Harold looked alarmed.

"I wouldn't bother with a detective," he said. "They don't know half as much as they pretend."

"I am inclined to agree with Harold," said Mrs.
Merton. "I will act as my own detective."

Save for the compliment to Harold, Mrs. Tracy
was not pleased with this speech of her aunt.

"At any rate," she said, "you would do well to
keep a strict watch over that boy, Luke Walton."

"I shall," answered the old lady, simply.

Mrs. Tracy looked triumphant. It was clear, she
thought, that Mrs. Merton was coming to her view
of the matter.

Warner kept silent, but a transient smile passed
over his face as he saw how neatly Aunt Eliza had
deceived his astute sister.

"What do you think, Warner?" asked Mrs.
Tracy, desirous of additional support.

"I think Aunt Eliza will get at the truth sooner
or later. Of course I will do anything to help her,
but I don't want to interfere."

"Don't you think she ought to discharge Luke?"

"If she did, she would have no chance of finding
out whether he was guilty or not."

"That is true. I did not think of that."

"Warner is more sensible than any of you," said
Mrs. Merton.

"I am glad you have changed your opinion of
him," said Mrs. Tracy, sharply.

She was now beginning to be jealous of her scapegrace brother.

"So am I," said Warner, smiling. "At the same
time, I don't blame aunt for her former opinion."

The next morning Harold was about leaving the house, when Felicie, the French maid, came up softly, and said: " Master Harold, may I have a word with you? "

" I am in a hurry," said Harold, impatiently.

" It is about the stolen money," continued Felicie, in her soft voice. " You had better listen to what I have to say. I have found out who took it."

Harold's heart gave a sudden thump, and his face indicated dismay.

CHAPTER XXXII

HAROLD AND FELICIE MAKE AN ARRANGEMENT

" You have found out who took the money?"
stammered Harold.

" Yes."

" I didn't think it would be found out so soon,"
said Harold, trying to recover his equanimity. " Of
course it was taken by Luke Walton."

" You are quite mistaken," said Felicie. " Luke
Walton did not take it."

Harold's heart gave another thump. He scented
danger, but remained silent.

" You don't ask me who took the money?" said
Felicie, after a pause.

" Because I don't believe you know," returned
Harold. " You've probably got some suspicion?"

" I have more than that. The person who took
the money was seen at his work."

Harold turned pale.

" There is no use in mincing matters," continued
Felicie. " You took the money!"

" What do you mean by such impertinence?"
gasped Harold.

"It is no impertinence. If you doubt my knowledge, I'll tell you the particulars. You opened the drawer with one of a bunch of keys which you took from your pocket, took out a morocco pocketbook, opened it, and counted the roll of bills which it contained, then put the pocketbook into your pocket, locked the drawer and left the room."

"That's a fine story," said Harold, forcing himself to speak. "I dare say all this happened, only you were the one who opened the drawer."

"I saw it all through a crack in the half-open door," continued Felicie, not taking the trouble to answer his accusation. "If you want further proof, suppose you feel in your pocket. I presume the pocketbook is there at this moment."

Instinctively Harold put his hand into his pocket, then suddenly withdrew it, as if his fingers were burned, for the pocketbook was there as Felicie had said.

"There is one thing more," said Felicie, as she drew from her pocket a bunch of keys. "I found this bunch of keys in your room this morning."

"They are not mine," answered Harold, hastily.

"I don't know anything about that. They are the ones you had in your hand when you opened the drawer. I think this is the key you used."

"The keys belong to you!" asserted Harold, desperately.

"Thank you for giving them to me, but I shall have no use for them," said Felicie, coolly. "And

now, Master Harold, do you want to know why I
have told you this little story?"

"Yes," answered Harold, feebly.

"Because I think it will be for our mutual advantage to come to an understanding. I don't want
to inform your aunt of what I have seen unless you
compel me to do so."

"How should I compel you to do so?" stammered Harold, uneasily.

"Step into the parlor, where we can talk com-
fortably. Your aunt is upstairs, and your mother
is out, so that no one will hear us."

Harold felt that he was in the power of the
cunning Felicie, and he followed her unresistingly.

"Sit down on the sofa, and we will talk at our
ease. I will keep silent about this matter, and no
one else knows a word about it, if——"

"Well?"

"If you will give me half the money."

"But," said Harold, who now gave up the pre-
tense of denial, "I have spent part of it."

"You have more than half of it left?"

"Yes."

"Give me thirty dollars and I will be content. I
saw you count it. There were sixty-five dollars."

"I don't see what claim you have to it," said
Harold, angrily.

"I have as much as you," answered Felicie,
coolly. "Still, if you prefer to go to your aunt, own
up that you took it, and take the consequences, I

will agree not to interfere. But if I am to keep the secret, I want to be paid for it."

Harold thought it over; he hated to give up so large a part of his plunder, for he had appropriated it in his own mind to certain articles which he wished to purchase.

"I'll give you twenty dollars," he said.

"No, I will take thirty dollars, or go to your aunt and tell her all I know."

There was no help for it. Poor Harold took out three ten-dollar bills, reluctantly enough, and gave them to Felicie.

"All right, Master Harold! You've done wisely. I thought you would see matters in the right light. Think how shocked your mother and Aunt Eliza would be if they had discovered that you were the thief."

"Don't use such language, Felicie!" said Harold, wincing. "There is no need to refer to it again."

"As you say, Master Harold. I won't detain you any longer from your walk," and Felicie, with a smile, rose from the sofa and left the room, Harold following.

"Don't disturb yourself any more," she said, as she opened the door for Harold. "It will never be known. Besides, your aunt can well afford to lose this little sum. She is actually rolling in wealth. She ought to be more liberal to you."

"So she ought, Felicie. If she had, this would not have happened."

"Very true. At the same time, I don't suppose
a jury would accept this as an excuse."

"Why do you say such things, Felicie? What
has a jury got to do with me?"

"Nothing, I hope. Still, if it were a poor boy
that had taken the money, Luke Walton, for instance, he might have been arrested. Excuse me, I
see this annoys you. Let me give you one piece of
advice, Master Harold."

"What is it?"

"Get rid of that morocco pocketbook as soon as
you can. If it were found on you, or you should be
careless, and leave it anywhere, you would give
yourself away, my friend."

"You are right, Felicie," said Harold, hurriedly.
"Good-morning!"

"Good-morning, and a pleasant walk, my friend,"
said Felicie, mockingly.

When Harold was fairly out in the street, he
groaned in spirit. He had lost half the fruits of
his theft, and his secret had become known. Felicie
had proved too much for him, and he felt that he
hated her.

"I wish I could get mother to discharge her,
without her knowing that it was I who had brought
it about. I shall not feel safe as long as she is in
the house. Why didn't I have the sense to shut and
lock the door? Then she wouldn't have seen me."

Then the thought of the morocco pocketbook
occurred to him. He felt that Felicie was right—

that it was imprudent to carry it around. He must get rid of it in some way.

He took the money out and put it in another pocket. The pocketbook he replaced till he should have an opportunity of disposing of it.

Hardly had he made these preparations when he met Luke Walton, who had started unusually early, and was walking towards the house. An idea came to Harold.

" Good-morning, Luke ! " he said, in an unusually friendly tone.

" Good-morning, Harold ! " answered Luke, agreeably surprised by the other's cordiality.

" Are you going out with Aunt Eliza this morning ? "

" I am not sure whether she will want to go out. I shall call and inquire."

" You seem to be quite a favorite of hers."

" I hope I am. She always treats me kindly."

" I really believe she thinks more of you than she does of me."

" You mustn't think that," said Luke, modestly. " You are a relation, and I am only in her employ."

" Oh, it doesn't trouble me. I am bound for the city. I think I shall take the next car—good-day ! "

" Good-day, Harold ! "

Luke walked on, quite unconscious that Harold, as he passed by his side, had managed to slip the morocco wallet into the pocket of his sack coat.

CHAPTER XXXIII

HAROLD'S PLOT FAILS

Luke wore a sack coat with side pockets. It was this circumstance that had made it easy for Harold to transfer the wallet unsuspected to his pocket.

Quite ignorant of what had taken place, Luke kept on his way to Mrs. Merton's house. He rang the bell, and on being admitted, went up, as usual, to the room of his patroness.

" Good-morning, Luke," said Mrs. Merton, pleasantly.

" Good-morning," responded Luke.

" I don't think I shall go out this morning, and I don't think of any commission, so you will have a vacation."

" I am afraid I am not earning my money, Mrs. Merton. You make it very easy for me."

" At any rate, Luke, the money is cheerfully given, and I have no doubt you find it useful. How are you getting along? "

" Very well, indeed! I have just made the last payment on mother's machine, and now we owe nothing, except, perhaps, for the rent, and only a week has gone by on the new month."

"You seem to be a good manager, Luke. You succeed in keeping your money, while I have not always found it easy. Yesterday, for instance, I lost sixty-five dollars."

"How was that?" inquired Luke, with interest.

"The drawer in which I keep a pocketbook was unlocked, and this, with its contents, was stolen."

"Don't you suspect anyone?"

"I did, but he has cleared himself, in my opinion. It is possible it was one of the servants."

At this moment Luke pulled the handkerchief from his side pocket, and with it came the morocco pocketbook, which fell on the carpet.

Mrs. Merton uttered an exclamation of surprise.

"Why, that is the very pocketbook!" she said.

Luke stooped and picked it up, with an expression of bewilderment on his face.

"I don't understand it," he said. "I never saw that pocketbook before in my life."

"Please hand it to me."

Luke did so.

"Yes, that is the identical pocketbook," said the old lady.

"And it came from my pocket?"

"Yes."

"Is there any money in it, Mrs. Merton?"

Mrs. Merton opened it, and shook her head.

"That has been taken out," she answered.

"I hope you won't think I took the money," said Luke, with a troubled look.

"I know you did not. It was taken while we were out together yesterday. The last thing before I left the house I locked the drawer, and the pocketbook with the money inside was there. When I returned it was gone."

"That is very mysterious. I don't understand how the pocketbook came in my pocket."

"Someone must have put it there who wished you to be suspected of the theft."

"Yes," said Luke, eagerly. "I see."

Then he stopped suddenly, for what he was about to say would throw suspicion upon Harold.

"Well, go on!"

"I don't know that I ought to speak. It might throw suspicion on an innocent person."

"Speak! it is due to me. I will judge on that point. Who has had the chance of putting the wallet into your pocket?"

"I will speak if you insist upon it, Mrs. Merton," said Luke, reluctantly. "A few minutes since I met Harold on the street. We were bound in opposite directions. He surprised me by stopping me, and addressing me quite cordially. We stood talking together two or three minutes."

"Did he have an opportunity of putting the wallet in your pocket?"

"He might have done so, but I was not conscious of it."

"Let me think!" said the old lady, slowly. "Harold knew where I kept my money, for I opened the drawer in his presence the other day, and he saw me take a bill from the pocketbook. I did not think him capable of robbing me."

"Perhaps he did not," said Luke. "It may be explained in some other way."

"Can you think of any other way?" asked the old lady.

"Suppose a servant had taken the money, and left the pocketbook somewhere where Harold found it——"

"Even in that case, why should he put it in your pocket?"

"He does not like me. He might wish to throw suspicion upon me."

"That would be very mean."

"I think it would, but still he might not be a thief."

"I would sooner excuse a thief. It is certainly disreputable to steal, but it is not necessarily mean or contemptible. Trying to throw suspicion on an innocent person would be both."

Luke remained silent, for nothing occurred to him to say. He did not wish to add to Mrs. Merton's resentment against Harold.

After a moment's thought the old lady continued: "Leave the pocketbook with me, and say nothing about what has happened till I give you leave."

"Very well."

Mrs. Merton took the pocketbook, replaced it in the drawer, and carefully locked it.

"Someone must have a key that will open this drawer," she said. "I should like to know who it is."

"Do you think anyone will open it again?" asked Luke.

"No; it will be supposed that I will no longer keep money there. I think, however, I will sooner or later find out who opened it."

"I hope it won't prove to be Harold."

"I hope so, too. I would not like to think so near a relative a thief. Well, Luke, I won't detain you here any longer. You may come to-morrow, as usual."

"It is lucky Mrs. Merton has confidence in me," thought Luke. "Otherwise she might have supposed me to be the thief. What a mean fellow Harold Tracy is, to try to have an innocent boy suspected of such a crime."

As he was going out of the front door, Mrs. Tracy entered.

She cast a withering glance at Luke.

"Have you seen my aunt this morning?" she asked.

"Yes, madam."

"I wonder you had the face to stand in her presence."

It must be said, in justification of Mrs. Tracy, that she really believed that Luke had stolen Mrs. Merton's money.

"I know of no reason why I should not," said

Luke, calmly. "Will you be kind enough to explain what you mean?"

"You know well enough," retorted Mrs. Tracy, nodding her head venomously.

"Mrs. Merton appears to be well satisfied with me," said Luke, quietly. "When she is not, she will tell me so, and I shall never come again."

"You are the most brazen boy I know of. Why it is that my aunt is so infatuated with you, I can't, for my part, pretend to understand."

"If you will allow me, I will bid you good-morning," said Luke, with quiet dignity.

Mrs. Tracy did not reply, and Luke left the house.

"If I ever hated and despised a boy, it is that one!" said Mrs. Tracy to herself, as she went upstairs to remove her street dress. "I wish I could strip the mask from him, and get aunt to see him in his real character. He is a sly, artful young adventurer. Ah, Felicie, come and assist me. By the way, I want you to watch that boy who has just gone out."

"Luke Walton?"

"Yes; of course you have heard of my aunt's loss. I suspect that this Luke Walton is the thief."

"Is it possible, madam? Have you any evidence?"

"No, but we may find some. What do you think?"

"I haven't thought much about the matter. It seems to me very mysterious."

When Felicie left the presence of her mistress, she smiled curiously.

"What would Madam Tracy say if she knew it was her own son?" she soliloquized. "He is a young cur, but she thinks him an angel!"

CHAPTER XXXIV

HAROLD MAKES A PURCHASE

Harold had been compelled to give up half his money, but he still had thirty dollars left. How should he invest it? That was the problem that occupied his thoughts. Thus far he had not derived so much satisfaction from the possession of the money as he had anticipated. One thing, at any rate, he resolved. He would not spend it upon others, but wholly upon himself.

He stepped into a billiard saloon to enjoy his favorite pastime. In the absence of any companion he played a game with a man employed in the establishment, and, naturally, got beaten, though he was given odds. At the end of an hour he owed sixty cents, and decided not to continue.

"You play too well for me," he said, in a tone of disappointment.

"You had bad luck," answered his opponent, soothingly. "However, I can more than make it up to you."

"How?" inquired Harold, becoming interested.

"A friend of mine has pawned his watch for fifteen dollars. It is a valuable gold watch—cost sev-

217

enty-five. He could have got more on it, but expected to redeem it. He has been in bad luck, and
finds it no use. He has put the ticket in my hands,
and is willing to sell it for ten dollars. That will
only make the watch cost twenty-five. It's a big
bargain for somebody."

Harold was much interested. He had always
wanted a gold watch, and had dropped more than
one hint to that effect within the hearing of Aunt
Eliza, but the old lady had always said: " When
you are eighteen, it will be time enough to think of
a gold watch. Till then, your silver watch will do."

Harold took a different view of the matter, and
his desire for a gold watch had greatly increased
since a school friend about his own age had become
the owner of one. For this reason he was considerably excited by the chance that seemed to present
itself.

" You are sure the watch is a valuable one? " he
asked.

" Yes; I have seen it myself."

" Then, why don't you buy the ticket yourself? "

" I haven't the money. If I had, I wouldn't let
anybody else have it."

" Let me see the ticket."

The other produced it from his vest pocket, but,
of course, this threw no light upon the quality of
the watch.

" I can secure the watch, and have nearly five
dollars left," thought Harold. " It is surely worth

double the price it will cost me, and then I shall have
something to show for my money."

On the other hand, his possession of the watch
would excite surprise at home, and he would be
called upon to explain how he obtained it. This,
however, did not trouble Harold. He was sure he
could make up a story that would avert suspicion.

"I've a great mind to take it," he said, slowly.

"You can't do any better. To tell the truth, I
hate to let it go, but I don't see any prospect of my
being able to get it out myself, and my friend needs
the money."

Harold hesitated a moment, then yielded to the
inducement offered.

"Give me the ticket," he said. "Here is the
money."

As he spoke, he produced a ten-dollar bill. In
return, the ticket was handed to him.

The pawnbroker, whose name he found on the
ticket, was located less than fifteen minutes' walk
from the billiard saloon. Harold, eager to secure
the watch, went directly there. Over the doorway
were displayed the customary three golden balls.

Entering with some nervousness, for he had never
before been in an establishment of this kind, Harold
advanced to the counter, behind which he saw
shelves loaded with articles in great variety.

"Well, young man, what can I do for you?"
asked a small man, with wrinkled face and blinking
eyes.

" I want to redeem my watch. Here is the ticket."

The old man glanced at the ticket, then went to a safe, and took out the watch. Here were kept the articles of small bulk and large value.

Harold took out fifteen dollars which he had put in his vest pocket for the purpose, and tendered them to the pawnbroker.

" I want a dollar and a half more," said the old man.

" What for? " asked Harold, in surprise.

" One month's interest. You don't think I do business for nothing, do you? "

" Isn't that high? " asked Harold, and not without reason.

" It's our regular charge, young man. Ten per cent. a month—that's what we all charge."

This statement was correct. Though the New York pawnbroker is allowed to charge but three per cent. a month, his Chicago associate charges more than three times as much.

There was nothing for it but to comply with the terms demanded, and Harold reluctantly handed out the extra sum.

" You ought to have a watch chain, my friend," said the pawnbroker.

" I should like one, but I cannot afford it."

" I can give you a superior article—rolled gold—for a dollar. It is just the amount I loaned on it, but I have had it for over a year, and the owner will never come after it."

"Let me see it!"

The chain was displayed. It looked very well; and certainly set off the watch to better advantage.

Harold paid down the dollar, and went out of the pawnbroker's with a gold watch, and chain of the same color, with only two dollars left of his ill-gotten money. This was somewhat inconvenient, but he rejoiced in the possession of the watch and chain.

"Now Ralph Kennedy can't crow over me," he soliloquized. "I've got a gold watch as well as he."

As he left the pawnbroker's, he did not observe a familiar face and figure on the opposite side of the street. It was Warner Powell, his mother's brother, who recognized, with no little surprise, his nephew, coming from such a place.

"What on earth has carried Harold to a pawnbroker's?" he asked himself.

Then he caught sight of the watch chain, and got a view of the watch, as Harold drew it out ostentatiously to view his new acquisition.

"There's some mystery here," he said to himself. "I must investigate."

He waited till Harold was at a safe distance, then crossed the street, and entered the pawnbroker's.

"There was a boy just went out of here," he said to the old man.

"Suppose there was," returned the pawnbroker, suspiciously.

"What was he doing here?"

"Is that any of your business?"

"My friend, I have nothing to do with you, and no complaint to make against you, but the boy is my nephew, and I want to know whether he got a watch and chain here."

"Yes; he presented a ticket, and I gave him the watch."

"Is it one he pawned himself?"

"I don't know. He had the ticket. I can't remember everybody that deals with me."

"Can you tell me how much the watch and chain were pawned for?"

"The watch was pawned for fifteen dollars. I sold him the chain for a dollar."

"All right! Thank you."

"It's all right?"

"Yes, so far as you are concerned. How long had the watch been in?"

"For three weeks."

"Thank you."

Warner Powell left the shop, after obtaining all the information he required.

"It is Harold who robbed Aunt Eliza," he said to himself. "He has done a very imprudent thing in securing this watch. I wonder what explanation he will have to give when he is asked about it at home. I begin to think my precious nephew is a rogue."

Meanwhile, Harold, eager to ascertain the value of his watch, stepped into a jeweler's.

"Can you tell me the value of this watcn?" he inquired.

The jeweler opened it, and after a brief examination, said: "When new it probably cost thirty-five dollars."

Harold's countenance fell.

"I was told that it was a seventy-five-dollar watch," he said.

"Then you were cheated."

"But how can such a large watch be afforded for thirty-five dollars?"

"It is low-grade gold, not over ten carats, and the works are cheap. Yet, it'll keep fair time."

Harold was very much disappointed. He had not made much of a bargain, after all.

CHAPTER XXXV

A SKILLFUL INVENTION

When he came to think it over, Harold gradually recovered his complacence. It was a gold watch, after all, and no one would know that the gold was low grade. He met one or two acquaintances, who immediately took notice of the chain and asked to see the watch. They complimented him on it, and this gave him satisfaction.

When he reached home, he went directly upstairs to his room, and only came down when he heard the supper bell.

As he entered the dining room his mother was the first to notice the watch chain.

"Have you been buying a watch chain, Harold?" she asked.

"I have something besides," said Harold, and he produced the watch.

Mrs. Tracy uttered an exclamation of surprise, and Mrs. Merton and Warner exchanged significant glances.

"How came you by the watch and chain?" asked Mrs. Tracy, uneasily.

"They were given to me," answered Harold

224

' But that is very strange. Aunt Eliza, you have not given Harold a watch, have you?"

" No, Louisa. I think a silver watch is good enough for a boy of his age."

" Why don't you ask me, Louisa?" said Warner, smiling.

" I don't imagine your circumstances will admit of such a gift."

" You are right. I wish they did. Harold, we are all anxious to know the name of the benevolent individual who has made you such a handsome present. If you think he has any more to spare, I should be glad if you would introduce me."

" I will explain," said Harold, glibly. " I was walking along Dearborn Street about two o'clock, when I saw a gentleman a little in advance of me. He had come from the Commercial Bank, I judge, for it was not far from there I came across him. By some carelessness he twitched a wallet stuffed with notes from his pocket. A rough-looking fellow sprang to get it, but I was too quick for him. I picked it up, and hurrying forward, handed it to the gentleman. He seemed surprised and pleased.

" ' My boy,' he said, ' you have done me a great service. That wallet contained fifteen hundred dollars. I should have lost it but for you. Accept this watch and chain as a mark of my deep gratitude.'

" With that, he took the watch from his pocket,

and handed it to me. I was not sure wnetner I
ought to take it, but I have long wanted a gold
watch, and he seemed well able to afford the gift,
so I took it."

Mrs. Tracy never thought of doubting this plausi-
ble story.

"Harold," she said, "I am proud of you. I think
there was no objection to accepting the watch.
What do you say, Aunt Eliza?"

"Let me look at the watch, Harold," said the old
lady, not replying to her niece's question.

Harold passed it over complacently. He rather
plumed himself on the ingenious story he had in-
vented.

"What do you think of it, Warner?" asked Mrs.
Merton, passing it to her nephew.

"It is rather a cheap watch for a rich man to
carry," answered Warner, taking it in his hand and
opening it.

"I am sure it is quite a handsome watch," said
Mrs. Tracy.

"Yes, it is large and showy, but it is low-grade
gold."

"Of course, I don't know anything about that,"
said Harold. "At any rate, it is gold and good
enough for me."

"No doubt of that," said the old lady, dryly.

"Rich men don't always carry expensive
watches," said Mrs. Tracy. "They are often plain
in their tastes."

"This watch is rather showy," said Warner. "It can't be called plain."

"At any rate, Harold has reason to be satisfied. I am glad he obtained the watch in so creditable a manner. If it had been your protégé, Aunt Eliza, I suspect he would have kept the money."

"I don't think so, Louisa," said Mrs. Merton, quietly. "I have perfect confidence in Luke's honesty."

"In spite of your lost pocketbook?"

"Yes; there is nothing to connect Luke with that."

Harold thought he ought to get the advantage of the trick played upon Luke in the morning.

"I don't know as I ought to say anything," he said, hesitating, "but I met Luke this morning, and if I am not very much mistaken, I saw in his pocket a wallet that looked very much like aunt's. You know he wears a sack coat, and has a pocket on each side."

Again Mrs. Merton and Warner exchanged glances.

"This is important!" said Mrs. Tracy, in excitement. "Did you speak to him on the subject?"

"No."

"Why not?"

"I thought he might be innocent, and I didn't want to bring a false charge against him."

"You are very considerate," said Mrs. Merton.

It was impossible to infer anything from her tone.

"That seems quite conclusive, Aunt Eliza," said Mrs. Tracy, triumphantly. "I am sure Warner will agree with me."

"As to that, Louisa," said her brother, "Harold is not certain it was aunt's lost pocketbook."

"But he thinks it was."

"Yes, I think it was——"

"For my own part, I have no doubt on the subject," said Mrs. Tracy, in a positive tone. "He is the person most likely to take the money, and this makes less proof needful."

"But, suppose, after all, he is innocent," suggested Warner.

"You seem to take the boy's side, Warner. I am surprised at you."

"I want him to have a fair chance, that is all. I must say that I have been favorably impressed by what I have seen of the boy."

"At any rate, I think Aunt Eliza ought to question him sternly, not accepting any evasion or equivocation. He has been guilty of base ingratitude."

"Supposing him to be guilty?"

"Yes, of course."

"I intend to investigate the matter," said the old lady. "What do you think, Harold? Do you think it probable that Luke opened my drawer, and took out the pocketbook?"

"It looks very much like it," said Harold.

"Certainly it does," said Mrs. Tracy, with emphasis.

"Suppose we drop the conversation for the time being," suggested the old lady. "Harold has not wholly gratified our curiosity as to the watch and chain. Do you know, Harold, who the gentleman is to whom you rendered such an important service?"

"No, Aunt Eliza, I did not learn his name."

"What was his appearance? Describe him."

"He was a tall man," answered Harold, in a tone of hesitation.

"Was he an old or a young man?"

"He was an old man with gray hair. He walked very erect."

"Should you know him again, if you saw him?"

"Yes, I think so."

"Then, perhaps, we may have an opportunity of ascertaining who he was. My broker will probably know him from your description."

"Why do you want to find out who he is?" asked Harold, uneasily. "Don't you think I ought to keep the watch?"

"I have a feeling of curiosity on the subject. As to keeping it, I don't think the gentleman will be likely to reclaim it."

"Of course not. Why should he?" said Mrs. Tracy. "He gave it freely, and it would be very strange if he wished it back."

Here the conversation dropped, much to Harold's relief. Warner accompanied his aunt from the room.

"What do you think of Harold's story, Warner." asked the old lady.

"It is very ingenious."

"But not true?"

"No; he got the watch and chain from a pawn-broker. I saw him come out of the shop, and going in, questioned the pawnbroker. He must have got the ticket somewhere."

"Then it seems that Harold is not only a thief, but a liar."

"My dear aunt, let us not be too hard upon him. This is probably his first offense. I feel like being charitable, for I have been in the same scrape."

"I can overlook theft more easily than his attempt to blacken the reputation of Luke," said Mrs. Merton, sternly.

CHAPTER XXXVI

WARNER POWELL STARTS ON A JOURNEY

Thanks to the liberal compensation received from Mrs. Merton, Luke was enabled to supply his mother and Bennie with all the comforts they required, and even to put by two dollars a week. This he did as a measure of precaution, for he did not know how long the engagement at the house on Prairie Avenue would last. If he were forced to fall back on his earnings as a newsboy, the family would fare badly. This might happen, for he found himself no nearer securing the favor of Harold and his mother. The manner of the latter was particularly unpleasant when they met, and Harold scarcely deigned to speak to him. On the other hand, Warner Powell showed himself very friendly. He often took the opportunity to join Luke when he was leaving the house, and chat pleasantly with him. Luke enjoyed his companionship, because Warner was able to tell him about Australia and California, with both of which countries Mrs. Tracy's brother was familiar.

"Mother," said Harold, one day, "Uncle Warner seems very thick with that newsboy. I have several times seen them walking together."

Mrs. Tracy frowned, for the news displeased her.

"I am certainly very much surprised. I should think my brother might find a more congenial and suitable companion than Aunt Eliza's hired boy. I will speak to him about it."

She accordingly broached the subject to Warner Powell, expressing herself with emphasis.

"Listen, Louisa," said Warner, "don't you think I am old enough to choose my own company?"

"It doesn't seem so," retorted Mrs. Tracy, with a smile.

"At any rate, I don't need any instructions on that point."

"As my guest, you certainly ought to treat me with respect."

"So I do. But I don't feel bound to let you regulate my conduct."

"You know what cause I have—we both have—to dislike this boy."

"I don't dislike him."

"Then you ought to."

"He is in Aunt Eliza's employment. While he remains so, I shall treat him with cordiality."

"You are blind as a mole!" said Mrs. Tracy, passionately. "You can't see that he is trying to work his way into aunt's affections."

"I think he has done so already. She thinks a great deal of him."

"When you find her remembering him in her will, you may come over to my opinion."

"She is quite at liberty to remember him in her will, so far as I am concerned. There will be enough for us, even if she does leave Luke a legacy."

"I see you are incorrigible. I am sorry I invited you to remain in my house."

"I was under the impression that it was Aunt Eliza's house. You are claiming too much, Louisa."

Mrs. Tracy bit her lip, and was compelled to give up her attempt to secure her brother's allegiance. She contented herself with treating him with formal politeness, abstaining from all show of cordiality. This was carried on so far that it attracted the attention of Mrs. Merton.

"What is the trouble between you and Louisa?" she asked one day.

Warner laughed.

"She thinks I am too intimate with your boy, Luke."

"I don't understand."

"I often walk with Luke either on his way to or from the house. Harold has reported this to his mother, and the result is a lecture as to the choice of proper companions from my dignified sister."

Mrs. Merton smiled kindly on her nephew.

"Then you don't propose to give up Luke?" she said.

"No; I like the boy. He is worth a dozen Harolds. Perhaps I ought not to say this, for Harold is my nephew and they say blood is thicker than water.

However, it is a fact, nevertheless, that I like Luke the better of the two."

"I shall not blame you for saying that, Warner," returned the old lady. "I am glad that one of the family, at least, is free from prejudice. To what do you attribute Louisa's dislike of Luke?"

"I think, aunt, you are shrewd enough to guess the reason without appealing to me."

"Still, I would like to hear it from your lips."

"In plain words, then, Louisa is afraid you will remember Luke in your will."

"She doesn't think I would leave everything to him, does she?"

"She objects to your leaving anything. If it were only five hundred dollars she would grudge it."

"Louisa was always selfish," said Mrs. Merton, quietly. "I have always known that. She is not wise, however. She does not understand that I am a very obstinate old woman, and am more likely to take my own way if opposed."

"That's right, aunt! You are entitled to have your own way, and I for one am the last to wish to interfere with you."

"You will not fare any the worse for that! And now, Warner, tell me what are your chances of employment?"

"I wished to speak to you about that, aunt. There is a gentleman in Milwaukee who has a branch office in Chicago, and I understand that he wants someone to represent him here. His present

agent is about to resign his position, and I think I
have some chance of obtaining the place. It will be
necessary for me, however, to go to Milwaukee to
see him in person."

" Go, then, by all means," said Mrs. Merton. " I
will defray your expenses."

" Thank you very much, aunt. You know that I
have little money of my own. But there is another
thing indispensable, and that I am afraid you would
not be willing to do for me."

" What is it, Warner? "

" I shall have charge of considerable money belonging to my employer, and I learn from the present agent that I shall have to get someone to give
bonds for me in the sum of ten thousand dollars."

" Very well! I am willing to stand your
security."

Warner looked surprised and gratified.

" Knowing how dishonestly I have acted in the
past? " he said.

" The past is past. You are a different man, I
hope and believe."

" Aunt Eliza, you shall never regret the generous
confidence you are willing to repose in me. It is
likely to open for me a new career, and to make a
new man of me."

" That is my desire, Warner. Let me add that I
am only following your own example. You have
refused to believe evil of Luke, unlike your sister,
and have not been troubled by the kindness I have

shown him. This is something I remember to your credit."

"Thank you, aunt. If you have been able to discover anything creditable in me, I am all the more pleased."

"How much will this position pay you, supposing you get it?"

"Two thousand dollars a year. To me that will be a competence. I shall be able to save one-half, for I have given up my former expensive tastes, and am eager to settle down to a steady and methodical business life."

"When do you want to go to Milwaukee, Warner?"

"I should like to go at once."

"Here is some money to defray your expenses."

Mrs. Merton opened her table drawer, and took out a roll of bills amounting to fifty dollars.

"I wish you good luck!" she said.

"Thank you, aunt! I shall take the afternoon train to Milwaukee, and sleep there to-night."

Warner Powell hastened to catch the train, and, at six o'clock in the evening, landed, with a large number of fellow passengers, in the metropolis of Wisconsin.

CHAPTER XXXVII

THOMAS BROWNING'S SECRET

Warner Powell had learned wisdom and prudence with his increasing years, and, instead of inquiring for the best hotel, was content to put up at a humbler hostelry, where he would be comfortable. He made the acquaintance on the cars of a New York drummer, with whom he became quite sociable.

" I suppose you have been in Milwaukee often," said Warner.

" I go there once a year—sometimes twice."

" Where do you stay? "

" At the Prairie Hotel. It is a comfortable house —two dollars a day."

" Just what I want. I will go there."

So, at quarter-past six, Warner Powell found himself in the office of the hotel. He was assigned a room on the third floor.

After making his toilet, he went down to supper. At the table with him were two gentlemen who, from their conversation, appeared to be residents of the city. They were discussing the coming municipal election.

" I tell you, Browning will be our mayor," said

one. "His reputation as a philanthropist will elect him."

"I never took much stock in his claims on that score."

"He belongs to all the charitable societies, and is generally an officer."

"That may be; but how much does he give himself?"

"I don't know. I suppose he is a liberal subscriber."

"He wants to give that impression, but the man is as selfish as the average. He is said to be a hard landlord, and his tenants get very few favors."

"I am surprised to hear that."

"He is trading on his philanthropy. It would be interesting to learn where his wealth came from. I should not be surprised if he were more smart than honest."

Warner Powell found himself getting interested in this Browning. Was he really a good man, who was unjustly criticised, or was he a sham philanthropist, as charged?

"After all, it doesn't concern me," he said to himself. "The good people of Milwaukee may choose whom they please for mayor so far as I am concerned."

After supper Warner stepped up to the cigar stand to buy a cigar. This, as the reader will remember, was kept by Jack King, an old California acquaintance of Thomas Browning, whose first appearance in our story was in the chaiacter of a tramp and would-be burglar.

"Is business good?" asked Warner, pleasantly.

"It is fair; but it seems slow to a man like myself, who has made a hundred dollars a day at the mines in California."

"I have been in California myself," said Powell, "but it was recently, and no such sums were to be made in my time."

"That is true. It didn't last with me. I have noticed that even in the flush times few brought much money away with them, no matter how lucky they were."

"There must be some exceptions, however."

"There were. We have a notable example in Milwaukee."

"To whom do you refer?"

"To Thomas Browning, the man who is up for mayor."

Jack King laughed.

"I've heard a lot of talk about that man. He's very honest and very worthy, I hear."

"They call him so," he answered.

"I am afraid you are jealous of that good man," said Warner, smiling.

"I may be jealous of his success, but not of his reputation or his moral qualities."

"Then you don't admire him as much as the public generally?"

"No, I know him too well."

"He is really rich, is he not?"

"Yes; that is, he is worth, perhaps, two hundred thousand dollars."

"That would satisfy me."

"Or me. But I doubt whether the money was creditably gained."

"Do you know anything about it? Were you an acquaintance of his?"

"Yes; I can remember him when he was only a rough miner. I never heard that he was very lucky, but he managed to take considerable money East with him."

Warner eyed Jack King attentively.

"You suspect something," he said, shrewdly.

"I do. There was one of our acquaintances who had struck it rich, and accumulated about ten thousand dollars. Browning was thick with him, and I always suspected that when he found himself on his deathbed, he intrusted all his savings to Butler——"

"I thought you were speaking of Browning?"

"His name was Butler then. He has changed it since. But, as I was saying, I think he intrusted his money to Browning to take home to his family."

"Well?"

"The question is, did Browning fulfill his trust, or keep the money himself?"

"That would come out, wouldn't it? The family would make inquiries."

"They did not know that the dying man had

money. He kept it to himself, for he wanted to go
home and give them an agreeable surprise. Butler
knew this, and, I think, he took advantage of it."

"That was contemptible. But can't it be ascertained? Is it known where the family lives? What
is the name?"

"Walton."

"Walton!" repeated Warner Powell, in surprise.

"Yes; do you know any family of that name?"

"I know a boy in Chicago named Luke Walton.
He is in the employ of my aunt. A part of his time
he spends in selling papers."

"Mr. Browning told me that Walton only left a
daughter, and that the family had gone to the East-
ern States."

"Would he be likely to tell you the truth—supposing he had really kept the money?"

"Perhaps not. What more can you tell me about
this boy?"

Powell's face lighted up.

"I remember now, he told me that his father died
in California."

"Is it possible?" said Jack King, excited. "I
begin to think I am on the right track. I begin to
think, too, that I can tell where Tom Butler got his
first start."

"And now he poses as a philanthropist?"

"Yes."

"And is nominated for mayor?"

"Yes, also."

"How are your relations with him?"

"They should be friendly, for he and I were comrades in earlier days, and once I lent him money when he needed it, but he has been puffed up by his prosperity, and takes very little notice of me. He had to do something for me when I first came to Milwaukee, but it was because he was afraid not to."

Meanwhile Warner Powell was searching his memory. Where and how had he become familiar with the name of Thomas Browning? At last it came to him.

"Eureka!" he exclaimed, in excitement.

"What does that mean? I don't understand French."

Warner smiled.

"It isn't French," he said; "but Greek, all the Greek I know. It means 'I have discovered'—the mystery of your old acquaintance."

"Explain, please!" said Jack King, his interest becoming intense.

"I have a friend in Chicago—Stephen Webb, a nephew of your philanthropist—who has been commissioned by his uncle to find out all he can about this newsboy, Luke Walton. He was speculating with me why his uncle should be so interested in an obscure boy."

"Had his uncle told him nothing?"

"No, except that he dropped a hint about knowing Luke's father."

"This Luke and his family are poor, you say?"

" Yes, you can judge that from his employment. He is an honest, manly boy, however, and I have taken a fancy to him. I hope it will turn out as you say. But nothing can be proved. This Browning will probably deny that he received money in trust from the dead father."

Jack King's countenance fell.

" When you go back to Chicago talk with the boy, and find out whether the family have any evidence that will support their claim. Then send the boy on to me, and we will see what can be done."

" I accept the suggestion with pleasure. But I will offer an amendment. Let us write the boy to come on at once, and have a joint consultation in his interest."

CHAPTER XXXVIII

FELICIE PROVES TROUBLESOME

We must return to Chicago for a short time before recording the incidents of Luke's visit to Milwaukee.

Though Harold had lost nearly half of his money through being compelled to divide with Felicie, he was, upon the whole, well satisfied with the way in which he had escaped from suspicion. He had his gold watch, and, as far as he knew, the story which he had told about it had not been doubted. But something happened that annoyed and alarmed him.

One day, when there was no one else in the house except the servants, Felicie intercepted him as he was going out.

"I want a word with you, Master Harold," she said.

"I am in a hurry, Felicie," replied Harold, who had conceived a dislike for the French maid.

"Still I think you can spare me a few minutes," went on Felicie, smiling in an unpleasant manner.

"Well, be quick about it," said Harold, impatiently.

"I have a sister who is very sick. She is a widow with two children, and her means are very small."

" Goodness, Felicie! What is all this to me? Of
course, I'm sorry for her, but I don't know her."

" She looks to me to help her," continued Felicie.

" Well, that's all right! I suppose you are going
to help her."

" There is the trouble, Master Harold. I have
no money on hand."

" Well, I'm sure that is unlucky, but why do you
speak to me about it?"

" Because," and here Felicie's eyes glistened, " I
know you obtained some money recently from your
aunt."

" Hush!" said Harold, apprehensively.

" But it's true."

" And it's true that you made me give you half
of it."

" It all went to my poor sister," said Felicie,
theatrically.

" I don't see what I have to do with that," said
Harold, not without reason.

" So that I kept none for myself. Now I am sure
you will open your heart, and give me five dollars
more."

" I never heard such cheek!" exclaimed Harold,
indignantly. " You've got half, and are not satisfied with that."

" But think of my poor sister!" said Felicie,
putting her handkerchief to her eyes, in which there
were no tears.

" Think of me!" exclaimed Harold, angrily.

"Then you won't give me the trifle I ask?"

"Trifle? I haven't got it."

"Where is it gone?"

"Gone to buy this watch. That took nearly the whole."

"It is indeed so? I thought you received it as a reward for picking up a pocketbook."

"I had to tell my aunt something. Otherwise they would ask me embarrassing questions."

"Ah, *quelle invention!*" exclaimed Felicie, playfully. "And you really have none of the money left?"

"No."

"Then—there is only one way."

"What is that?"

"To open the drawer again."

"Are you mad, Felicie? I should surely be discovered. It won't do to try it a second time when my aunt is on her guard. Besides, very likely she don't keep her money there now."

"Oh, yes, she does."

"How do you know?"

"I was in the room yesterday when she opened the drawer to take out money to pay a bill."

"She must be foolish, then."

"Ah," said Felicie, coolly, "she thinks lightning won't strike twice in the same place."

"Well, it won't."

"There must have been fifty dollars in bills in the drawer," continued Felicie, insinuatingly.

"It may stay there for all me. I won't go to the drawer again."

"I must have some money," said Felicie, significantly.

"Then tell Aunt Eliza, and she may give you some."

"I don't think your Aunt Eliza likes me," said Felicie, frankly.

"Very likely not," said Harold, with equal candor.

"You can raise some money on your watch, Master Harold," suggested Felicie.

"How?"

"At the pawnbroker's."

"Well, I don't mean to."

"No?"

"No!" returned Harold, emphatically.

"Suppose I go and tell Mrs. Merton who took her money?"

"You would only expose yourself."

"I did not take it."

"You made me divide with you."

"I shall deny all that. Besides, I shall tell all that I saw—on that day."

Harold felt troubled. Felicie might, as he knew, make trouble for him, and though he could in time inform against her, that would not make matters much better for him. Probably the whole story would come out, and he felt sure that the French maid would not spare him.

A lucky thought came to him.

"Felicie," he said, "I think I can suggest something that will help you."

"Well, what is it?"

"Go to my aunt's drawer yourself. You have plenty of chance, and you can keep all the money you find. I won't ask you for any of it."

Felicie eyed him sharply. She was not sure but he meant to trap her.

"I have no keys," she said.

"You can use the same bunch I have. Here they are!"

Felicie paused a moment, then took the proffered keys. After all, why should she not make use of the suggestion? It would be thought that the second thief was the same as the first.

"Can I rely on your discretion, Master Harold?" she asked.

"Yes, certainly. I am not very likely to say anything about the matter."

"True! It might not be for your interest. Good-morning, Master Harold, I won't detain you any longer."

Harold left the house with a feeling of relief.

"I hope Felicie will be caught!" he said to himself. "I have a great mind to give Aunt Eliza a hint."

It looked as if the generally astute Felicie had made a mistake.

CHAPTER XXXIX

LUKE WALTON'S LETTER

" Here is a letter for you, Luke! " said Mrs. Walton.

Luke took it in his hand, and regarded it curiously. He was not in the habit of receiving letters.

" It is postmarked Milwaukee," he said.

" Do you know anyone in Milwaukee? " asked his mother.

" No; or stay, it must be from Mr. Powell, a brother of Mrs. Tracy."

" Probably he sends a message to his sister."

By this time Luke had opened the following letter, which he read with great surprise and excitement:

" DEAR LUKE: Come to Milwaukee as soon as you can, and join me at the Prairie Hotel. I write in your own interest. There is a large sum due to your father, which I may be able to put you in the way of collecting. You had better see Aunt Eliza, and ask leave of absence for a day or two. If you

249

haven't money enough to come on, let her know, and I am sure she will advance it to you.

"Your friend,

"WARNER POWELL."

"What can it mean?" asked Mrs. Walton, to whom Luke read the letter.

"It must refer to the ten thousand dollars which father sent to us on his dying bed."

"If it only were so!" said the widow, clasping her hands.

"At any rate, I shall soon find out, mother. I had better take the letter which was sent us, giving us the first information of the legacy."

"Very well, Luke! I don't know anything about business. I must leave the matter entirely in your hands."

"I will go at once to Mrs. Merton and ask if it will inconvenience her if I go away for a couple of days."

"Do so, Luke! She is a kind friend, and you should do nothing without her permission."

Luke took the cars for Prairie Avenue, though it was afternoon, and he had been there once already. He was shown immediately into the old lady's presence.

Mrs. Merton saw him enter with surprise.

"Has anything happened, Luke?" she asked.

"I have received a letter from your nephew, summoning me to Milwaukee."

"I hope he is not in any scrape."

"No; it is a very friendly letter, written in my interest. May I read it to you?"

"I shall be glad to hear it."

Mrs. Merton settled herself back in her rocking-chair, and listened to the reading of the letter.

"Do you know what this refers to, Luke?" she asked.

"Yes; my father on his deathbed in California intrusted a stranger with ten thousand dollars to bring to my mother. He kept it for his own use, and it was only by an accident that we heard about the matter."

"You interest me, Luke. What was the accident?"

Luke explained.

"It must be this that Mr. Powell refers to," he added.

"But I don't see how my nephew should have anything to do with it."

"There is a man in Milwaukee who answers the description of the stranger to whom my poor father intrusted his money. I have seen him, for he often comes to Chicago. I have even spoken to him."

"Have you ever taxed him with this breach of trust?"

"No, for he bears a different name. He is Thomas Browning, while the letter mentions Thomas Butler."

"He may have changed his name."

"I was stupid not to think of that before. There can hardly be two men so singularly alike. I have come to ask you, Mrs. Merton, if you can spare me for two or three days."

"For as long as you like, Luke," said the old lady, promptly. "Have you any money for your traveling expenses?"

"Yes, thank you."

"No matter. Here are twenty dollars. Money never comes amiss."

"You are always kind to me, Mrs. Merton," said Luke, gratefully.

"It is easy to be kind if one is rich. I want to see that man punished. Let me give you one piece of advice. Be on your guard with this man! He is not to be trusted."

"Thank you! I am sure your advice is good."

"I wish you good luck, Luke. However things may turn out, there is one thing that gratifies me. Warner is showing himself your friend. I have looked upon him till recently as a black sheep, but he is redeeming himself rapidly in my eyes. I shall not forget his kindness to you."

As Luke went downstairs he met Mrs. Tracy.

"Here again!" said she, coldly. "Did my aunt send for you this afternoon?"

"No, madam."

"Then you should not have intruded. You are young, but you are very artful. I see through your schemes, you may rest assured."

"I wished to show Mrs. Merton a letter from your brother, now in Milwaukee," said Luke.

"Oh, that's it, is it? Let me see the letter."

"I must refer you to Mrs. Merton."

"He has probably sent to Aunt Eliza for some money," thought Mrs. Tracy. "He and the boy are well matched."

CHAPTER XL

FACE TO FACE WITH THE ENEMY

Thomas Browning sat in his handsome study, in a complacent frame of mind. The caucus was to be held in the evening, and he confidently expected the nomination for mayor. It was the post he had coveted for a long time. There were other honors that were greater, but the mayoralty would perhaps prove a stepping-stone to them. He must not be impatient. He was only in middle life, and there was plenty of time.

"I didn't dream this when I was a penniless miner in California," he reflected, gleefully. "Fortune was hard upon me then, but now I am at the top of the heap. All my own good management, too. Tom Butler—no, Browning—is no fool, if I do say it myself."

"Someone to see you, Mr. Browning," said the servant.

"Show him in!" replied the philanthropist.

A poorly dressed man followed the maid into the room.

Mr. Browning frowned. He had thought it might be some influential member of his party.

"What do you want?" he asked, roughly.

The poor man stood humbly before him, nervously pressing the hat between his hands.

"I am one of your tenants, Mr. Browning. I am behindhand with my rent, owing to sickness in the family, and I have been ordered out."

"And very properly, too!" said Browning, "You can't expect me to let you stay gratis."

"But, sir, you have the reputation of being a philanthropist. It hardly seems in character——"

"I do not call myself a philanthropist—others call me so—and perhaps they are right. I help the poor to the extent of my means, but even a philanthropist expects his honest dues."

"Then you can do nothing for me, sir?"

"No; I do not feel called upon to interfere in your case."

The poor man went out sorrowfully, leaving the philanthropist in an irritable mood. Five minutes later a second visitor was announced.

"Who is it?" asked Browning, fearing it might be another tenant.

"It is a boy, sir."

"With a message, probably. Show him up."

But Thomas Browning was destined to be surprised, when in the manly-looking youth who entered he recognized the Chicago newsboy who had already excited his uneasiness.

"What brings you here?" he demanded, in a startled tone.

"I don't know if you remember me, Mr. Browning," said Luke, quietly. "I have sold you papers near the Sherman House, in Chicago."

"I thought your face looked familiar," said Browning, assuming an indifferent tone. "You have made a mistake in coming to Milwaukee. You cannot do as well here as in Chicago."

"I have not come here in search of a place. I have a good one at home."

"I suppose you have some object in coming to this city?"

"Yes; I came to see you."

"Upon my word, I ought to feel flattered, but I can't do anything for you. I have some reputation in charitable circles, but I have my hands full here."

"I have not come to ask you a favor, Mr. Browning. If you will allow me, I will ask your advice in a matter of importance to me."

Browning brightened up. He was always ready to give advice.

"Go on!" he said.

"When I was a young boy my father went to California. He left my mother, my brother, and myself very poorly provided for, but he hoped to earn money at the mines. A year passed, and we heard of his death."

"A good many men die in California," said Browning, phlegmatically.

"We could not learn that father left anything,

and we were compelled to get along as we could. Mother obtained sewing to do at low prices, and I sold papers."

"A common experience!" said Browning, coldly.

"About three months ago," continued Luke, "we were surprised by receiving, in a letter from a stranger, a message from my father's deathbed."

Thomas Browning started and turned pale, as he gazed intently in the boy's face.

"How much does he know?" he asked himself, apprehensively.

"Go on!" he said, slowly.

"In this letter we learned for the first time that father had intrusted the sum of ten thousand dollars to an acquaintance to be brought to my mother. This man proved false and kept the money."

"This story may or may not be true," said Browning, with an effort. "Was the man's name given?"

"Yes; his name was Thomas Butler."

"Indeed! Have you ever met him?"

"I think so," answered Luke, slowly. "I will read his description from the letter: 'He has a wart on the upper part of his right cheek—a mark which disfigures and mortifies him exceedingly. He is about five feet ten inches in height, with a dark complexion and dark hair, a little tinged with gray.'"

"Let me see the letter," said Browning, hoarsely.

He took the letter in his hand, and, moving near the grate fire, began to read it. Suddenly the paper,

as if accidentally, slipped from his fingers, and fell
upon the glowing coals—where it was instantly
consumed.

"How careless I am!" ejaculated Browning, but
there was exultation in the glance.

CHAPTER XLI

MR. BROWNING COMES TO TERMS

The destruction of the letter, and the open exultation of the man who had in intention at least doubly
wronged him, did not appear to dismay Luke Walton. He sat quite cool and collected, facing Mr.
Browning.

"Really, I don't see how this letter happened to
slip from my hand," continued the philanthropist.
"I am afraid you consider it important."

"I should if it had been the genuine letter," said
Luke.

"What?" gasped Browning.

"It was only a copy, as you will be glad to hear."

"Boy, I think you are deceiving me," said Browning, sharply.

"Not at all! I left the genuine letter in the hands
of my lawyer."

"Your lawyer?"

"Yes. I have put this matter in the hands of Mr.
Jordan, of this city."

Mr. Browning looked very much disturbed. Mr.
Jordan was a well-known and eminent attorney.
Moreover, he was opposed in politics to the would-be

mayor. If his opponent should get hold of this discreditable chapter in his past history, his political aspirations might as well be given up. Again he asked himself, " How much of the story does this boy know? "

" If you are employing a lawyer," he said, after a pause, " I don't understand why you came to me for advice."

" I thought you might be interested in the matter," said Luke, significantly.

" Why should I be interested in your affairs? I have so many things to think of that really I can't take hold of anything new."

" I will tell you, sir. You are the man who received money in trust from my dying father. I look to you to restore it with interest."

" How dare you insinuate any such thing? " demanded Browning, furiously. " Do you mean to extort money by threats? "

" No, sir. I only ask for justice."

" There is nothing to connect me with the matter. According to your letter it was a Thomas Butler who received the money you refer to."

" True, and your name at that time was Thomas Butler."

Mr. Browning turned livid. The net seemed to be closing about him.

" What proof have you of this ridiculous assertion? " he demanded.

" The testimony of one who knew you then and

now—Mr. King, who keeps a cigar stand at the Prairie Hotel."

"Ha! traitor!" ejaculated Browning, apostrophizing the absent King.

"This is a conspiracy!" he said. "King has put you up to this. He is a discreditable tramp whom I befriended when in dire need. This is my reward for it."

"I have nothing to do with that, Mr. Browning. Mr. King is ready to help me with his testimony. My lawyer has advised me to call upon you, and to say this: If you will pay over the ten thousand dollars with interest I will engage in my mother's name to keep the matter from getting before the public."

"And if I don't agree to this?"

"Mr. Jordan is instructed to bring suit against you."

Drops of perspiration gathered on the brow of Mr. Browning. This would never do. The suit, even if unsuccessful, would blast his reputation as a philanthropist, and his prospects as a politician.

"I will see Mr. Jordan," he said.

"Very well, sir. Then I wish you good-morning."

Within two days Thomas Browning had paid over to the lawyer for his young client the full sum demanded, and Luke left Milwaukee with the happy consciousness that his mother was now beyond the reach of poverty.

CHAPTER XLII

CONCLUSION

Felicie reflected over Harold's dishonest suggestion, and concluded to adopt it. She meant to charge Harold with the second robbery, and to brazen it out if necessary. Accordingly, one day she stole into Mrs. Merton's sitting room, and with the keys supplied by Harold succeeded in opening the drawer. Inside, greatly to her surprise, she saw the identical pocketbook which it had been understood was taken at the time of the first robbery. She was holding it in her hand, when a slight noise led her to look up swiftly.

To her dismay she saw the old lady, whom she had supposed out of the house, regarding her sternly.

"What does this mean, Felicie?" demanded Mrs. Merton.

"I—I found these keys and was trying them to see if any of them had been used at the time your money was stolen."

"Do you know who took my money on that occasion?" continued the old lady.

"Yes, I do," answered Felicie, swiftly deciding to tell the truth.

"Who was it?"

"Your nephew Harold," answered Felicie, glibly.

"You know this?"

"I saw him open the drawer. I was looking through a crack of the door."

"And you never told me of this?"

"I didn't want to expose him. He begged me not to do so."

"That is singular. He warned me yesterday that he suspected you of being the thief, and that he had reason to think you were planning a second robbery."

"He did?" said Felicie, with flashing eyes.

"Yes; what have you to say to it?"

"That he put me up to it, and gave me these keys to help me in doing it. Of course, he expected to share the money."

This last statement was untrue, but Felicie was determined to be revenged upon her treacherous ally.

"And you accepted?"

"Yes," said Felicie, seeing no way of escape. "I am poor, and thought you wouldn't miss the money."

"My nephew accused Luke Walton of being the thief."

"It is untrue. He wanted to divert suspicion from himself. Besides, he hates Luke."

"Do you?"

"No; I think him much better than Harold."

"So do I. Where did my nephew get his gold watch?"

"It was bought with the money he stole from the drawer."

"So I supposed. Well, Felicie, you can go, but I think you had better hand me that bunch of keys."

"Shall you report me to Mrs. Tracy?"

"I have not decided. For the present we will both keep this matter secret."

Luke's absence was, of course, noticed by Mrs. Tracy.

"Have you discharged Luke Walton?" she asked, hopefully. "I observe he has not come here for the last two or three days."

"He has gone out of the city—on business."

"I am surprised that you should trust that boy to such an extent."

At this moment a telegraph messenger rang the bell, and a telegram was brought up to Mrs. Merton. It ran thus:

"To MRS. MERTON, —— Prairie Avenue, Chicago:

"I have recovered all my mother's money with interest. Mr. Powell is also successful. Will return this evening. LUKE WALTON."

"Read it if you like, Louisa," said the old lady, smiling with satisfaction.

"What does it mean?"

"That Luke has recovered over ten thousand dollars, of which his mother had been defrauded. It was Warner who put him on the track of the man who wrongfully held the money."

"Indeed!" said Mrs. Tracy, spitefully. "Then the least he can do is to return the money he took from you."

"He never took any, Louisa."

"Who did, then?"

"Your son Harold."

"Who has been telling lies about my poor boy?" exclaimed Mrs. Tracy, angrily.

"A person who saw him unlocking the drawer."

"Has Luke Walton been telling falsehoods about my son?"

"No; it was quite another person. I have othr proof also, and have known for some time who the real thief was. If Harold claims that I have done him injustice, send him to me."

After an interview with Harold, Mrs. Tracy was obliged to believe, much against her will, that he was the guilty one and not the boy she so much detested. This did not prepossess her any more in favor of Luke Walton, whom she regarded as the rival and enemy of her son.

It was a joyful coming home for Luke. He removed at once to a nice neighborhood, and ceased to be a Chicago newsboy. He did not lose the friendship of Mrs. Merton, who is understood to have put him down for a large legacy in her will, and still employs him to transact much of her busi-

ness. Next year she proposes to establish her
nephew, Warner Powell, and Luke in a commission
business, under the style of

POWELL & WALTON,

she furnishing the capital.

The house on Prairie Avenue is closed. Mrs.
Tracy is married again, to a man whose intem-
perate habits promise her little happiness. Harold
seems unwilling to settle down to business, but has
developed a taste for dress and the amusements of
a young man about town. He thinks he will even-
tually be provided for by Mrs. Merton, but in this
he will be mistaken, as she has decided to leave
much the larger part of her wealth to charitable
institutions after remembering her nephew, Warner
Powell, handsomely.

Ambrose Kean never repeated the mistake he had
made. Still more, by diligent economy he saved up
the sum advanced him by Mrs. Merton, and he
offered it to her. She accepted it, but returned it
many times over to his mother. Her patronage
brought him another advantage; it led his employer
to increase his salary, which is now double that
which he formerly received.

Felicie lost her position, but speedily secured
another, where it is to be hoped she will be more
circumspect in her conduct.

Thomas Browning, after all, lost the nomination

which he craved—and much of his wealth is gone. He dabbled in foolish speculations, and is now comparatively a poor man. Through the agency of Jack King, the story of his breach of trust was whispered about, and the sham philanthropist is better understood and less respected by his fellow-citizens.

His nephew, Stephen Webb, has been obliged to buckle down to hard work at ten dollars a week, and feels that his path is indeed thorny.

Luke Walton is not puffed up by his unexpected and remarkable success. He never fails to recognize kindly, and help, if there is need, the old associates of his humbler days, and never tries to conceal the fact that he was once a Chicago newsboy.

THE END

A PIPE OF MYSTERY.

A JOVIAL party were gathered round a blazing fire in an old grange near Warwick. The hour was getting late; the very little ones had, after dancing round the Christmas-tree, enjoying the snap-dragon, and playing a variety of games, gone off to bed; and the elder boys and girls now gathered round their uncle, Colonel Harley, and asked him for a story— above all, a ghost story.

"But I have never seen any ghosts," the colonel said, laughing; "and, moreover, I don't believe in them one bit. I have traveled pretty well all over the world, I have slept in houses said to be haunted, but nothing have I seen—no noises that could not be accounted for by rats or the wind have I ever heard. I have never"—and here he paused—"never but once met with any circumstances or occurrence that could not be accounted for by the light of reason, and I know you prefer hearing stories of my own adventures to mere invention."

"Yes, uncle. But what was the 'once' when circumstances happened that you could not explain?"

"It's rather a long story," the colonel said, "and it's getting late."

"Oh! no, no, uncle; it does not matter a bit how late we sit up on Christmas Eve, and the longer the story is, the better; and if you don't believe in ghosts how can it be a story of something you could not account for by the light of nature?"

"You will see when I have done," the colonel said. "It is rather a story of what the Scotch call second sight, than one of ghosts. As to accounting for it, you shall form your own opinion when you have heard me to the end.

"I landed in India in '50, and after going through the regular drill work marched with a detachment up country to join my regiment, which was stationed at Jubbalpore, in the very heart of India. It has become an important place since; the railroad across India passes through it and no end of changes have taken place; but at that time it was one of the most out-of-the-way stations in India, and, I may say, one of the most pleasant. It lay high, there was capital boating on the Nerbudda, and, above all, it was a grand place for sport, for it lay at the foot of the hill country, an immense district, then but little known, covered with forests and jungle, and abounding with big game of all kinds.

"My great friend there was a man named Simmonds. He was just of my own standing; we had come out in the same ship, had marched up the country together, and were almost like brothers. He was an old Etonian, I an old Westminster, and we were both fond of boating, and, indeed, of sport of all kinds. But I am not going to tell you of that now. The people in these hills are called Gonds, a true hill tribe—that is to say, aborigines, somewhat of the negro type. The chiefs are of mixed blood, but the people are almost black. They are supposed to accept the religion of the Hindus, but are in reality deplorably ignorant and superstitious. Their priests are a sort of compound of a Brahmin priest and a negro fetish man, and among their principal duties is that of charming away tigers from the villages by means of incantations. There, as in other parts of India, were a few wandering fakirs, who enjoyed an immense reputation for holiness and wisdom. The people would go to them from great distances for charms or predictions, and believed in their power with implicit faith.

"At the time when we were at Jubbalpore there was one of these fellows whose reputation altogether eclipsed that of his rivals, and nothing could be done until his permission had been asked and his blessing obtained. All sorts of marvelous stories were constantly coming to our ears of the unerring foresight with which he predicted the termination of diseases, both in men and animals; and so generally was he believed in that the colonel ordered that no one connected with the regiment should consult him, for these predictions very frequently brought about their own fulfillment; for those who were told that an illness would terminate fatally, lost all hope, and literally lay down to die.

"However, many of the stories that we heard could not be explained on these grounds, and the fakir and his doings were often talked over at mess, some of the officers scoffing at the whole business, others maintaining that some of these fakirs had, in some way or another, the power of foretelling the future, citing many well-authenticated anecdotes upon the subject.

"The older officers were the believers, we young fellows were the scoffers. But for the well-known fact that it is very seldom indeed that these fakirs will utter any of their predictions to Europeans, some of us would have gone to him to test his powers. As it was, none of us had ever seen him.

"He lived in an old ruined temple, in the middle of a large patch of jungle at the foot of the hills, some ten or twelve miles away.

"I had been at Jubbalpore about a year, when I was woke up one night by a native, who came in to say that at about eight o'clock a tiger had killed a man in his village, and had dragged off the body.

"Simmonds and I were constantly out after tigers, and the people in all the villages within twenty miles knew that we were always ready to pay for early information. This tiger had been doing great damage, and had carried off about thirty men, women, and children. So great was the fear of him, indeed, that the people in the neighborhood he frequented scarcely dared stir out of doors, except in parties of five or six. We had had several hunts after him, but, like all man-eaters, he was old and awfully crafty; and although we got several snap shots at him, he had always managed to save his skin.

"In a quarter of an hour after the receipt of the message Charley Simmonds and I were on the back of an elephant which was our joint property; our shikaree, a capital fellow, was on foot beside us, and with the native trotting on ahead as guide we went off at the best pace of old Begaum, for that was the elephant's name. The village was fifteen miles away, but we got there soon after daybreak, and were received with delight by the population. In half an hour the hunt was organized; all the male population turned out as beaters, with sticks, guns, tom-toms, and other instruments for making a noise.

"The trail was not difficult to find. A broad path, with occasional smears of blood, showed where he had dragged his victim through the long grass to a cluster of trees a couple of hundred yards from the village.

"We scarcely expected to find him there, but the villagers held back, while we went forward with cocked rifles. We found, however, nothing but a few bones and a quantity of blood. The tiger had made off at the approach of daylight into the jungle, which was about two miles distant. We traced him easily enough, and found that he had entered a large ravine, from which several smaller ones branched off.

"It was an awkward place, as it was next to impossible to surround it with the number of people at our command. We posted them at last all along the upper ground, and told them to make up in noise what they wanted in numbers. At last all was ready, and we gave the signal. However, I am not telling you a hunting story, and need only say that we could neither find nor disturb him. In vain we pushed Begaum through the thickest of the jungle which clothed the sides and bottom of the ravine, while the men shouted, beat their tom-toms, and showered imprecations against the tiger himself and his ancestors up to the remotest generations.

"The day was tremendously hot, and, after three hours' march, we gave it up for a time, and lay down in the shade, while the shikarees made a long examination of the ground all round the hillside, to be sure that he had not left the ravine. They came back with the news that no traces could be discovered, and that, beyond a doubt, he was still there. A tiger will crouch up in an exceedingly small clump of grass or bush, and will sometimes almost allow himself to be trodden on before moving. However, we determined to have one more search, and if that should prove unsuccessful, to send off to Jubbalpore for some more of the men to come out with elephants, while we kept up a circle of fires, and of noises of all descriptions, so as to keep him a prisoner until the arrival of the re-enforcements. Our next search was no more successful than our first had been; and having, as we imagined, examined every clump and crevice in which he could have been concealed, we had just reached the upper end of the ravine, when we heard a tremendous roar, followed by a perfect babel of yells and screams from the natives.

"The outburst came from the mouth of the ravine, and we felt at once that he had escaped. We hurried back to find, as we had expected, that the tiger was gone. He had burst out suddenly from his hiding-place, had seized a native, torn him horribly, and had made across the open plain.

"This was terribly provoking, but we had nothing to do but follow him. This was easy enough, and we traced him to a detached patch of wood and jungle, two miles distant. This wood was four or five hundred yards across, and the exclamations of the people at once told us that it was the one in which stood the ruined temple of the fakir of whom I have been telling you. I forgot to say that as the tiger broke out one of the village shikarees had fired at and, he declared, wounded him.

"It was already getting late in the afternoon, and it was hopeless to attempt to beat the jungle that night. We therefore sent off a runner with a note to the colonel, asking him to send the work-elephants, and to allow a party of volunteers to march over at night, to help surround the jungle when we commenced beating it in the morning.

"We based our request upon the fact that the tiger was a notorious man-eater, and had been doing immense damage. We then had a talk with our shikaree, sent a man off to bring provisions for the people out with us, and then set them to work cutting dry sticks and grass to make a circle of fires.

"We both felt much uneasiness respecting the fakir, who might be seized at any moment by the enraged tiger. The natives would not allow that there was any cause for fear, as the tiger would not dare to touch so holy a man. Our belief in the respect of the tiger for sanctity was by no means strong, and we determined to go in and warn him of the presence of the brute in the wood. It was a mission which we could not intrust to anyone else, for no native would have entered the jungle for untold gold; so we mounted the Begaum again, and started. The path leading towards the temple was pretty wide, and as we went along almost noiselessly, for the elephant was too well trained to tread upon fallen sticks, 't was just possible we might come upon the tiger suddenly, so we kept our rifles in readiness in our hands.

"Presently we came in sight of the ruins. No one was at first visible; but at that very moment the fakir came out from the temple. He did not see or hear us, for we were rather behind him and still among the trees, but at once proceeded in a high voice to break into a sing-song prayer. He had not said two words before his voice was drowned in a terrific roar, and in an instant the tiger had sprung upon him, struck him to the ground, seized him as a cat would a mouse, and started off with him at a trot. The brute evidently had not detected our presence, for he came right towards us. We halted the Begaum, and, with our fingers on the triggers, awaited the favorable moment. He was a hundred yards from us when he struck down his victim; he was not more than fifty when he caught sight of us. He stopped for an instant in surprise. Charley muttered, 'Both barrels, Harley,' and as the beast turned to plunge into the jungle, and so showed us his side, we sent four bullets crashing into him, and he rolled over lifeless.

"We went up to the spot, made the Begaum give him a kick, to be sure that he was dead, and then got down to examine the unfortunate fakir. The tiger had seized him by the shoulder, which was terribly torn, and the bone broken. He was still perfectly conscious.

"We at once fired three shots, our usual signal that the tiger was dead, and in a few minutes were surrounded by the villagers, who hardly knew whether to be delighted at the death of their enemy, or to grieve over the injury to the fakir. We proposed taking the latter to our hospital at Jubbalpore, but this he positively refused to listen to. However, we finally persuaded him to allow his arm to be set and the wounds dressed in the first place by our regimental surgeon, after which he could go to one of the native villages and have his arm dressed in accordance with his own notions. A litter was soon improvised, and away we went to Jubbalpore, which we reached about eight in the evening.

"The fakir refused to enter the hospital, so we brought out a couple of trestles, laid the litter upon them, and the surgeon set his arm and dressed his wounds by torchlight, when he was lifted into a dhoolie, and his bearers again prepared to start for the village.

"Hitherto he had only spoken a few words; but he now briefly expressed his deep gratitude to Simmonds and myself. We told him that we would ride over to see him shortly, and hoped to find him getting on rapidly. Another minute and he was gone.

"It happened that we had three or four fellows away on leave or on staff duty, and several others laid up with fever just about this time, so that the duty fell very heavily upon the rest of us, and it was over a month before we had time to ride over to see the fakir.

"We had heard he was going on well; but we were surprised, on reaching the village, to find that he had already returned to his old abode in the jungle. However, we had made up our minds to see him, especially as we had agreed that we would endeavor to persuade him to do a prediction for us; so we turned our horses' heads towards the jungle. We found the fakir sitting on a rock in front of the temple, just where he had been seized by the tiger. He rose as we rode up.

"'I knew that you would come to-day, sahibs, and was joyful in the thought of seeing those who have preserved my life.'

"'We are glad to see you looking pretty strong again, though your arm is still in a sling,' I said, for Simmonds was not strong in Hindustani.

"'How did you know that we were coming?' I asked, when we had tied up our horses.

"'Siva has given to his servant to know many things,' he said quietly.

"'Did you know beforehand that the tiger was going to seize you?' I asked.

"'I knew that a great danger threatened, and that Siva would not let me die before my time had come.'

"'Could you see into our future?' I asked.

" The fakir hesitated, looked at me for a moment
earnestly to see if I was speaking in mockery, and
then said:

" ' The sahibs do not believe in the power of Siva
or of his servants. They call his messengers im-
postors, and scoff at them when they speak of the
events of the future.'

" ' No indeed,' I said. ' My friend and I have
no idea of scoffing. We have heard of so many of
your predictions coming true, that we are really anxious that you should tell us something of the future.'

" The fakir nodded his head, went into the temple,
and returned in a minute or two with two small pipes
used by the natives for opium-smoking, and a brazier
of burning charcoal. The pipes were already
charged. He made signs to us to sit down, and took
his place in front of us. Then he began singing in
a low voice, rocking himself to and fro, and waving
a staff which he held in his hand. Gradually his
voice rose, and his gesticulations and actions became
more violent. So far as I could make out, it was a
prayer to Siva that he would give some glimpse of
the future which might benefit the sahibs who had
saved the life of his servant. Presently he darted
forward, gave us each a pipe, took two pieces of red-
hot charcoal from the brazier in his fingers, without
seeming to know that they were warm, and placed
them in the pipes; then he recommenced his singing
and gesticulations.

"A glance at Charley, to see if, like myself, he was ready to carry the thing through, and then I put the pipe to my lips. I felt at once that it was opium, of which I had before made experiment, but mixed with some other substance, which was, I imagine, hasheesh, a preparation of hemp. A few puffs, and I felt a drowsiness creeping over me. I saw, as through a mist, the fakir swaying himself backwards and forwards, his arms waving and his face distorted. Another minute, and the pipe slipped from my fingers, and I fell back insensible.

"How long I lay there I do not know. I woke with a strange and not unpleasant sensation, and presently became conscious that the fakir was gently pressing, with a sort of shampooing action, my temples and head. When he saw that I opened my eyes he left me, and performed the same process upon Charley. In a few minutes he rose from his stooping position, waved his hand in token of adieu, and walked slowly back into the temple.

"As he disappeared I sat up; Charley did the same.

"We stared at each other for a minute without speaking, and then Charley said:

"'This is a rum go, and no mistake, old man.'

"'You're right, Charley. My opinion is, we've made fools of ourselves. Let's be off out of this.'

"We staggered to our feet, for we both felt like drunken men, made our way to our horses, poured

a mussuk of water over our heads, took a drink of
brandy from our flasks, and then, feeling more like
ourselves, mounted and rode out of the jungle.

" 'Well, Harley, if the glimpse of futurity which
I had is true, all I can say is that it was extremely
unpleasant.'

" 'That was just my case, Charley.'

" 'My dream, or whatever you like to call it, was
about a mutiny of the men.'

" 'You don't say so, Charley; so was mine. This
is monstrously strange, to say the least of it. However, you tell your story first, and then I will tell
mine.'

" 'It was very short,' Charley said. 'We were
at mess—not in our present mess-room—we were
dining with the fellows of some other regiment.
Suddenly, without any warning, the windows were
filled with a crowd of Sepoys, who opened fire right
and left into us. Half the fellows were shot down
at once; the rest of us made a rush to our swords
just as the niggers came swarming into the room.
There was a desperate fight for a moment. I remember that Subadar Pirán—one of the best native
officers in the regiment, by the way—made a rush
at me, and I shot him through the head with a revolver. At the same moment a ball hit me, and
down I went. At the moment a Sepoy fell dead
across me, hiding me partly from sight. The fight
lasted a minute or two longer. I fancy a few fel-

lows escaped, for I heard shots outside. Then the
place became quiet. In another minute I heard a
crackling, and saw that the devils had set the mess-
room on fire. One of our men, who was lying close
by me, got up and crawled to the window, but he
was shot down the moment he showed himself. I
was hesitating whether to do the same or to lie still
and be smothered, when suddenly I rolled the dead
Sepoy off, crawled into the anteroom half-suffocated
by smoke, raised the lid of a very heavy trapdoor,
and stumbled down some steps into a place, half-
storehouse half cellar, under the mess-room. How
I knew about it being there I don't know. The trap
closed over my head with a bang. That is all I remember.'

" ' Well, Charley, curiously enough my dream was
also about an extraordinary escape from danger,
lasting, like yours, only a minute or two. The first
thing I remember—there seems to have been something before, but what, I don't know—I was on
horseback, holding a very pretty but awfully pale
girl in front of me. We were pursued by a whole
troop of Sepoy cavalry, who were firing pistol-shots
at us. We were not more than seventy or eighty
yards in front, and they were gaining fast, just as I
rode into a large deserted temple. In the center was
a huge stone figure. I jumped off my horse with
the lady, and as I did so she said, "blow out my
brains, Edward; don't let me fall into their hands."

" ' Instead of answering, I hurried her round behind the idol, pushed against one of the leaves of a flower in the carving, and the stone swung back, and showed a hole just large enough to get through, with a stone staircase inside the body of the idol, made, no doubt, for the priest to go up and give responses through the mouth. I hurried the girl through, crept in after her, and closed the stone, just as our pursuers came clattering into the courtyard. That is all I remember.'

" ' Well, it is monstrously rum,' Charley said, after a pause. ' Did you understand what the old fellow was singing about before he gave us the pipes ? '

" ' Yes; I caught the general drift. It w; ; an entreaty to Siva to give us some glimpse of futurity which might benefit us.'

" We lit our cheroots and rode for some miles at a brisk canter without remark. When we were within a short distance of home we reined up.

" ' I feel ever so much better,' Charley said. ' We have got that opium out of our heads now. How do you account for it all, Harley ? '

" ' I account for it in this way, Charley. The opium naturally had the effect of making us both dream, and as we took similar doses of the same mixture, under similar circumstances, it is scarcely extraordinary that it should have effected the same portion of the brain, and caused a certain similarity in our dreams. In all nightmares something terrible happens, or is on the point of happening; and so it was here. Not unnaturally in both our cases our thoughts turned to soldiers. If you remember, there was a talk at mess some little time since as to what would happen in the extremely unlikely event of the Sepoys mutinying in a body. I have no doubt that was the foundation of both our dreams. It is all natural enough when we come to think it over calmly. I think, by the way, we had better agree to say nothing at all about it in the regiment.'

" ' I should think not,' Charley said. ' We should never hear the end of it; they would chaff us out of our lives.'

" We kept our secret, and came at last to laugh over it heartily when we were together. Then the subject dropped, and by the end of a year had as much escaped our minds as any other dream would have done. Three months after the affair the regiment was ordered down to Allahabad, and the change of place no doubt helped to erase all memory of the dream. Four years after we had left Jubbalpore we went to Beerapore. The time is very marked in my memory, because, the very week we arrived there, your aunt, then Miss Gardiner, came out from England, to her father, our colonel. The instant I saw her I was impressed with the idea that I knew her intimately. I recollected her face, her figure, and the very tone of her voice, but wherever

I had met her I could not conceive. Upon the occasion of my first introduction to her I could not
help telling her that I was convinced that we had
met, and asking her if she did not remember it. No,
she did not remember, but very likely she might have
done so, and she suggested the names of several
people at whose houses we might have met. I did
not know any of them. Presently she asked how
long I had been out in India?

" ' Six years,' I said.

" ' And how old, Mr. Harley,' she said, ' do you
take me to be? '

" I saw in one instant my stupidity, and was
stammering out an apology, when she went on:

" ' I am very little over eighteen, Mr. Harley, although I evidently look ever so many years older;
but papa can certify to my age; so I was only twelve
when you left England.'

" I tried in vain to clear matters up. Your aunt
would insist that I took her to be forty, and the fun
that my blunder made rather drew us together, and
gave me a start over the other fellows at the station,
half of whom fell straightway in love with her.
Some months went on, and when the mutiny broke
out we were engaged to be married. It is a proof
of how completely the opium-dreams had passed out
of the minds of both Simmonds and myself, that
even when rumors of general disaffection among the
Sepoys began to be current, they never once recurred

to us; and even when the news of the actual mutiny reached us we were just as confident as were the others of the fidelity of our own regiment. It was the old story, foolish confidence and black treachery. As at very many other stations, the mutiny broke out when we were at mess. Our regiment was dining with the 34th Bengalees. Suddenly, just as dinner was over, the window was opened, and a tremendous fire poured in. Four or five men fell dead at once, and the poor colonel, who was next to me, was shot right through the head. Everyone rushed to his sword and drew his pistol—for we had been ordered to carry pistols as part of our uniform. I was next to Charley Simmonds as the Sepoys of both regiments, headed by Subadar Pirán, poured in at the windows.

" ' I have it now,' Charley said; ' it is the scene I dreamed.'

" As he spoke he fired his revolver at the subadar, who fell dead in his tracks.

" A Sepoy close by leveled his musket and fired. Charley fell, and the fellow rushed forward to bayonet him. As he did so I sent a bullet through his head, and he fell across Charley. It was a wild fight for a minute or two, and then a few of us made a sudden rush together, cut our way through the mutineers, and darted through an open window on to the parade. There were shouts, shots, and screams from the officers' bungalows, and in several places flames were already rising. What became of the other men I knew not; I made as hard as I could tear for the colonel's bungalow. Suddenly I came upon a sowar sitting on his horse watching the rising flames. Before he saw me I was on him, and ran him through. I leapt on his horse and galloped down to Gardiner's compound. I saw lots of Sepoys in and around the bungalow, all engaged in looting. I dashed into the compound.

"'May! May!' I shouted. 'Where are you?'

"I had scarcely spoken before a dark figure rushed out of a clump of bushes close by with a scream of delight.

"In an instant she was on the horse before me, and, shooting down a couple of fellows who made a rush at my reins, I dashed out again. Stray shots were fired after us. But fortunately the Sepoys were all busy looting, most of them had laid down their muskets, and no one really took up the pursuit. I turned off from the parade-ground, dashed down between the hedges of two compounds, and in another minute we were in the open country.

"Fortunately, the cavalry were all down looting their own lines, or we must have been overtaken at once. May happily had fainted as I lifted her on to my horse—happily, because the fearful screams that we heard from the various bungalows almost drove me mad, and would probably have killed her, for the poor ladies were all her intimate friends.

"I rode on for some hours, till I felt quite safe from any immediate pursuit, and then we halted in the shelter of a clump of trees.

"By this time I had heard May's story. She had felt uneasy at being alone, but had laughed at herself for being so, until upon her speaking to one of the servants he had answered in a tone of gross insolence, which had astonished her. She at once guessed that there was danger, and the moment that she was alone caught up a large, dark carriage rug, wrapped it round her so as to conceal her white dress, and stole out into the veranda. The night was dark, and scarcely had she left the house than she heard a burst of firing across at the mess-house. She at once ran in among the bushes and crouched there, as she heard the rush of men into the room she had just left. She heard them searching for her, but they were looking for a white dress, and her dark rug saved her. What she must have suffered in the five minutes between the firing of the first shots and my arrival, she only knows. May had spoken but very little since we started. I believe that she was certain that her father was dead, although I had given an evasive answer when she asked me; and her terrible sense of loss, added to the horror of that time of suspense in the garden, had completely stunned her. We waited in the tope until the afternoon, and then set out again.

"We had gone but a short distance when we saw

a body of the rebel cavalry in pursuit. They had no
doubt been scouring the country generally, and the
discovery was accidental. For a short time we kept
away from them, but this could not be for long, as
our horse was carrying double. I made for a sort of
ruin I saw at the foot of a hill half a mile away. I
did so with no idea of the possibility of concealment.
My intention was simply to get my back to a rock
and to sell my life as dearly as I could, keeping the
last two barrels of the revolver for ourselves. Certainly no remembrance of my dream influenced me
in any way, and in the wild whirl of excitement I
had not given a second thought to Charley Simmonds' exclamation. As we rode up to the ruins
only a hundred yards ahead of us, May said:

"'Blow out my brains, Edward; don't let me fall
alive into their hands.'

"A shock of remembrance shot across me. The
chase, her pale face, the words, the temple—all my
dream rushed into my mind.

"'We are saved,' I cried, to her amazement, as
we rode into the courtyard, in whose center a great
figure was sitting.

"I leapt from the horse, snatched the mussuk of
water from the saddle, and then hurried May round
the idol, between which and the rock behind there
was but just room to get along.

"Not a doubt entered my mind but that I should
find the spring as I had dreamed. Sure enough

there was the carving, fresh upon my memory as if I had seen it but the day before. I placed my hand on the leaflet without hesitation, a solid stone moved back, I hurried my amazed companion in, and shut to the stone. I found, and shot to, a massive bolt, evidently placed to prevent the door being opened by accident or design when anyone was in the idol.

"At first it seemed quite dark, but a faint light streamed in from above; we made our way up the stairs, and found that the light came through a number of small holes pierced in the upper part of the head, and through still smaller holes lower down, not much larger than a good-sized knitting-needle could pass through. These holes, we afterwards found, were in the ornaments round the idol's neck. The holes enlarged inside, and enabled us to have a view all round.

"The mutineers were furious at our disappearance, and for hours searched about. Then, saying that we must be hidden somewhere, and that they would wait till we came out, they proceeded to bivouac in the courtyard of the temple.

"We passed four terrible days, but on the morning of the fifth a scout came in to tell the rebels that a column of British troops marching on Delhi would pass close by the temple. They therefore hastily mounted and galloped off.

"Three-quarters of an hour later we were safe among our own people. A fortnight afterwards your aunt and I were married. It was no time for ceremony then; there were no means of sending her away; no place where she could have waited until the time for her mourning for her father was over. So we were married quietly by one of the chaplains of the troops, and, as your story-books say, have lived very happily ever after."

"And how about Mr. Simmonds, uncle? Did he get safe off too?"

"Yes, his dream came as vividly to his mind as mine had done. He crawled to the place where he knew the trapdoor would be, and got into the cellar. Fortunately for him there were plenty of eatables there, and he lived there in concealment for a fortnight. After that he crawled out, and found the mutineers had marched for Delhi. He went through a lot, but at last joined us before that city. We often talked over our dreams together, and there was no question that we owed our lives to them. Even then we did not talk much to other people about them, for there would have been a lot of talk, and inquiry, and questions, and you know fellows hate that sort of thing. So we held our tongues. Poor Charley's silence was sealed a year later at Lucknow, for on the advance with Lord Clyde he was killed.

"And now, boys and girls, you must run off to bed. Five minutes more and it will be Christmas Day. So you see, Frank, that although I don't be-

fieve in ghosts, I have yet met with a circumstance
which I cannot account for."

" It is very curious anyhow, uncle, and beats ghost
stories into fits."

" I like it better, certainly," one of the girls said,
" for we can go to bed without being afraid of
dreaming about it."

" Well, you must not talk any more now. Off to
bed, off to bed," Colonel Harley said, " or I shall
get into terrible disgrace with your fathers and
mothers, who have been looking very gravely at me
for the last three-quarters of an hour."

WHITE-FACED DICK.

How Pine-tree Gulch got its name no one knew, for in the early days every ravine and hillside was thickly covered with pines. It may be that a tree of exceptional size caught the eye of the first explorer, that he camped under it, and named the place in its honor; or, may be, some fallen giant lay in the bottom and hindered the work of the first prospectors. At any rate, Pine-tree Gulch it was, and the name was as good as any other. The pine-trees were gone now. Cut up for firing, or for the erection of huts, or the construction of sluices, but the hillside was ragged with their stumps.

The principal camp was at the mouth of the Gulch, where the little stream, which scarce afforded water sufficient for the cradles in the dry season, but which was a rushing torrent in winter, joined the Yuba. The best ground was at the junction of the streams, and lay, indeed, in the Yuba Valley rather than in the Gulch. At first most gold had been found higher up, but there was here comparatively little depth down to the bed-rock, and as the ground became ex-

hausted the miners moved down towards the mouth
of the Gulch. They were doing well, as a whole,
how well no one knew, for miners are chary of giving information as to what they are making; still, it
was certain they were doing well, for the bars were
doing a roaring trade, and the storekeepers never refused credit—a proof in itself that the prospects were
good.

The flat at the mouth of the Gulch was a busy
scene, every foot was good-paying stuff, for in the
eddy, where the torrents in winter rushed down into
the Yuba, the gold had settled down and lay thick
among the gravel. But most of the parties were
sinking, and it was a long way down to the bed-rock;
for the hills on both sides sloped steeply, and the
Yuba must here at one time have rushed through
a narrow gorge, until, in some wild freak, it brought
down millions of tons of gravel, and resumed its
course seventy feet above its former level.

A quarter of a mile higher up a ledge of rock ran
across the valley, and over it in the old time the
Yuba had poured in a cascade seventy feet deep into
the ravine. But the rock now was level with the
gravel, only showing its jagged points here and there
above it. This ledge had been invaluable to the
diggers: without it they could only have sunk their
shafts with the greatest difficulty, for the gravel
would have been full of water, and even with the
greatest pains in puddling and timber-work the

pumps would scarcely have sufficed to keep it down as it rose in the bottom of the shafts. But the miners had made common cause together, and giving each so many ounces of gold or so many days' work had erected a dam thirty feet high along the ledge of rock, and had cut a channel for the Yuba along the lower slopes of the valley. Of course, when the rain set in, as everybody knew, the dam would go, and the river diggings must be abandoned till the water subsided and a fresh dam was made; but there were two months before them yet, and everyone hoped to be down to the bed-rock before the water interrupted their work.

The hillside, both in the Yuba Valley and for some distance along Pine-tree Gulch, was dotted by shanties and tents; the former constructed for the most part of logs roughly squared, the walls being some three feet in height, on which the sharp sloping roof was placed, thatched in the first place with boughs, and made all snug, perhaps, with an old sail stretched over all. The camp was quiet enough during the day. The few women were away with their washing at the pools, a quarter of a mile up the Gulch, and the only persons to be seen about were the men told off for cooking for their respective parties.

But in the evening the camp was lively. Groups of men in red shirts and corded trousers tied at the knee, in high boots, sat round blazing fires, and talked of their prospects or discussed the news of the

luck at other camps. The sound of music came
from two or three plank erections which rose con-
spicuously above the huts of the diggers, and were
bright externally with the glories of white and colored paints. To and from these men were always
sauntering, and it needed not the clink of glasses and
the sound of music to tell that they were the bars of
the camp.

Here, standing at the counter, or seated at
numerous small tables, men were drinking villainous
liquor, smoking and talking, and paying but scant
attention to the strains of the fiddle or the accordion,
save when some well-known air was played, when all
would join in a boisterous chorus. Some were always passing in or out of a door which led into a
room behind. Here there was comparative quiet,
for men were gambling, and gambling high.

Going backwards and forwards with liquors into
the gambling-room of the Imperial Saloon, which
stood just where Pine-tree Gulch opened into Yuba
Valley, was a lad, whose appearance had earned for
him the name of White-faced Dick.

White-faced Dick was not one of those who had
done well at Pine-tree Gulch; he had come across the
plains with his father, who had died when halfway
over, and Dick had been thrown on the world to shift
for himself. Nature had not intended him for the
work, for he was a delicate, timid lad; what spirits
he originally had having been years before beaten

out of him by a brutal father. So far, indeed, Dick
was the better rather than the worse for the event
which had left him an orphan.

They had been traveling with a large party for
mutual security against Indians and Mormons, and
so long as the journey lasted Dick had got on fairly
well. He was always ready to do odd jobs, and as
the draught cattle were growing weaker and weaker,
and every pound of weight was of importance, no
one grudged him his rations in return for his services; but when the company began to descend the
slopes of the Sierra Nevada they began to break up,
going off by twos and threes to the diggings of
which they heard such glowing accounts. Some,
however, kept straight on to Sacramento, determin-
ing there to obtain news as to the doings at all the
different places, and then to choose that which
seemed to them to offer the surest prospects of
success.

Dick proceeded with them to the town, and there
found himself alone. His companions were absorbed in the busy rush of population, and each had
so much to provide and arrange for, that none gave
a thought to the solitary boy. However, at that
time no one who had a pair of hands, however feeble,
to work need starve in Sacramento, and for some
weeks Dick hung around the town doing odd jobs,
and then, having saved a few dollars, determined to
try his luck at the diggings, and started on foot with

a shovel on his shoulders and a few days' provisions slung across it.

Arrived at his destination, the lad soon discovered that gold-digging was hard work for brawny and seasoned men, and after a few feeble attempts in spots abandoned as worthless he gave up the effort, and again began to drift; and even in Pine-tree Gulch it was not difficult to get a living. At first he tried rocking cradles, but the work was far harder than it appeared. He was standing ankle-deep in water from morning till night, and his cheeks grew paler, and his strength, instead of increasing, seemed to fade away. Still, there were jobs within his strength. He could keep a fire alight and watch a cooking-pot, he could carry up buckets of water or wash a flannel shirt, and so he struggled on, until at last some kind-hearted man suggested to him that he should try to get a place at the new saloon which was about to be opened.

" You are not fit for this work, young 'un, and you ought to be at home with your mother; if you like I will go up with you this evening to Jeffries. I knew him down on the flats, and I dare say he will take you on. I don't say as a saloon is a good place for a boy, still you will always get your bellyful of victuals and a dry place to sleep in, if it's only under a table. What do you say? "

Dick thankfully accepted the offer, and on Red George's recommendation was that evening engaged. His work was not hard now, for till the miners knocked off there was little doing in the saloon; a few men would come in for a drink at dinner-time, but it was not until the lamps were lit that business began in earnest, and then for four or five hours Dick was busy.

A rougher or healthier lad would not have minded the work, but to Dick it was torture; every nerve in his body thrilled whenever rough miners cursed him for not carrying out their orders more quickly, or for bringing them the wrong liquors, which, as his brain was in a whirl with the noise, the shout-ing, and the multiplicity of orders, happened fre-quently. He might have fared worse had not Red George always stood his friend, and Red George was an authority in Pine-tree Gulch—powerful in frame, reckless in bearing and temper, he had been in a score of fights and had come off them, if not un-scathed, at least victorious. He was notoriously a lucky digger, but his earnings went as fast as they were made, and he was always ready to open his belt and give a bountiful pinch of dust to any mate down on his luck.

"One evening Dick was more helpless and con-fused than usual. The saloon was full, and he had been shouted at and badgered and cursed until he scarcely knew what he was doing. High play was going on in the saloon, and a good many men were clustered round the table. Red George was having

a run of luck, and there was a big pile of gold dust
on the table before him. One of the gamblers who
was losing had ordered old rye, and instead of bringing it to him, Dick brought a tumbler of hot liquor
which someone else had called for. With an oath
the man took it up and threw it in his face.

"You cowardly hound!" Red George exclaimed.
"Are you man enough to do that to a man?"

"You bet," the gambler, who was a new arrival at
Pine-tree Gulch, replied; and picking up an empty
glass, he hurled it at Red George. The bystanders
sprang aside, and in a moment the two men were
facing each other with outstretched pistols. The
two reports rung out simultaneously: Red George
sat down unconcernedly with a streak of blood flow-
ing down his face, where the bullet had cut a furrow
in his cheek; the stranger fell back with a bullet
hole in the center of his forehead.

The body was carried outside, and the play continued as if no interruption had taken place. They
were accustomed to such occurrences in Pine-tree
Gulch, and the piece of ground at the top of the hill,
that had been set aside as a burial place, was already
dotted thickly with graves, filled in almost every instance by men who had died, in the local phraseology,
"with their boots on."

Neither then nor afterwards did Red George
allude to the subject to Dick, whose life after this
signal instance of his championship was easier than

It had hitherto been, for there were few in Pine-tree Gulch who cared to excite Red George's anger; and strangers going to the place were sure to receive a friendly warning that it was best for their health to keep their tempers over any shortcomings on the part of White-faced Dick.

Grateful as he was for Red George's interference on his behalf, Dick felt the circumstance which had ensued more than anyone else in the camp. With others it was the subject of five minutes' talk, but Dick could not get out of his head the thought of the dead man's face as he fell back. He had seen many such frays before, but he was too full of his own troubles for them to make much impression upon him. But in the present case he felt as if he himself was responsible for the death of the gambler; if he had not blundered this would not have happened.

He wondered whether the dead man had a wife and children, and, if so, were they expecting his return? Would they ever hear where he had died, and how?

But this feeling, which, tired out as he was when the time came for closing the bar, often prevented him from sleeping for hours, in no way lessened his gratitude and devotion towards Red George, and he felt that he could die willingly if his life would benefit his champion. Sometimes he thought, too, that his life would not be much to give, for, in spite of shelter and food, the cough which he had caught while working in the water still clung to him, and, as his employer said to him angrily one day:

"Your victuals don't do you no good, Dick; you get thinner and thinner, and folks will think as I starve you. Darned if you aint a disgrace to the establishment."

The wind was whistling down the gorges, and the clouds hung among the pine-woods which still clothed the upper slopes of the hills, and the diggers, as they turned out one morning, looked up apprehensively.

"But it could not be," they assured each other. Everyone knew that the rains were not due for another month yet; it could only be a passing shower if it rained at all.

But as the morning went on, men came in from camps higher up the river, and reports were current that it had been raining for the last two days among the upper hills; while those who took the trouble to walk across to the new channel could see for themselves at noon that it was filled very nigh to the brim, the water rushing along with thick and turbid current. But those who repeated the rumors, or who reported that the channel was full, were summarily put down. Men would not believe that such a calamity as a flood and the destruction of all their season's work could be impending. There had been some showers, no doubt, as there had often been before, but it was ridiculous to talk of anything like rain a month before its time. Still, in spite of these assertions, there was uneasiness at Pine-tree Gulch, and men looked at the driving clouds above and shook their heads before they went down to the shafts to work after dinner.

When the last customer had left and the bar was closed, Dick had nothing to do till evening, and he wandered outside and sat down on a stump, at first looking at the work going on in the valley, then so absorbed in his own thoughts that he noticed nothing, not even the driving mist which presently set in. He was calculating that he had, with his savings from his wages and what had been given him by the miners, laid by eighty dollars. When he got another hundred and twenty he would go; he would make his way down to San Francisco, and then by ship to Panama and up to New York, and then west again to the village where he was born. There would be people there who would know him, and who would give him work for his mother's sake. He did not care what it was; anything would be better than this.

Then his thoughts came back to Pine-tree Gulch, and he started to his feet. Could he be mistaken? Were his eyes deceiving him? No; among the stones and bowlders of the old bed of the Yuba there was the gleam of water, and even as he watched it he could see it widening out. He started to run down the hill to give the alarm, but before he was halfway he paused, for there were loud shouts, and a scene of bustle and confusion instantly arose.

The cradles were deserted, and the men working on the surface loaded themselves with their tools and made for the high ground, while those at the windlasses worked their hardest to draw up their comrades below. A man coming down from above stopped close to Dick, with a low cry, and stood gazing with a white scared face. Dick had worked with him; he was one of the company to which Red George belonged.

"What is it, Saunders?"

"My God! they are lost!" the man replied. "I was at the windlass when they shouted up to me to go up and fetch them a bottle of rum. They had just struck it rich, and wanted a drink on the strength of it."

Dick understood at once. Red George and his mates were still in the bottom of the shaft, ignorant of the danger which was threatening them.

"Come on," he cried; "we shall be in time yet," and at the top of his speed dashed down the hill, followed by Saunders.

"What is it, what is it?" asked parties of men mounting the hill.

"Red George's gang are still below."

Dick's eyes were fixed on the water. There was a broad band now of yellow with a white edge down the center of the stony flat, and it was widening with terrible rapidity. It was scarce ten yards from the windlass at the top of Red George's shaft when Dick, followed closely by Saunders, reached it.

"Come up, mates; quick, for your lives! The river is rising; you will be flooded out directly. Everyone else has gone!"

As he spoke he pulled at the rope by which the bucket was hanging, and the handles of the windlass flew round rapidly as it descended. When it had run out Dick and he grasped the handles

"All right below?"

An answering call came up, and the two began their work, throwing their whole strength into it. Quickly as the windlass revolved it seemed an endless time to Dick before the bucket came up, and the first man stepped out. It was not Red George. Dick had hardly expected it would be. Red George would be sure to see his two mates up before him, and the man uttered a cry of alarm as he saw the water, now within a few feet of the mouth of the shaft.

It was a torrent now, for not only was it coming through the dam, but it was rushing down in cascades from the new channel. Without a word the miner placed himself facing Dick, and the moment the bucket was again down, the three grasped the handles. But quickly as they worked, the edge of the water was within a few inches of the shaft when the next man reached the surface; but again the

bucket descended before the rope tightened. However, the water had begun to run over the lip—at
first, in a mere trickle, and then, almost instan-
taneously, in a cascade, which grew larger and
larger.

The bucket was halfway up when a sound like
thunder was heard, the ground seemed to tremble
under their feet, and then at the turn of the valley
above, a great wave of yellow water, crested with
foam, was seen tearing along at the speed of a race-
horse.

" The dam has burst! " Saunders shouted. " Run
for your lives, or we are all lost! "

The three men dropped the handles and ran at full
speed towards the shore, while loud shouts to Dick
to follow came from the crowd of men standing on
the slope. But the boy grasped the handles,
and with lips tightly closed, still toiled on. Slowly
the bucket ascended, for Red George was a heavy
man; then suddenly the weight slackened, and the
handle went round faster. The shaft was filling,
the water had reached the bucket, and had risen to
Red George's neck, so that his weight was no longer
on the rope. So fast did the water pour in, that it
was not half a minute before the bucket reached the
surface, and Red George sprang out. There was
but time for one exclamation, and then the great
wave struck them. Red George was whirled like a
straw in the current; but he was a strong swimmer,

and at a point where the valley widened out, half a mile lower, he struggled to shore.

Two days later the news reached Pine-tree Gulch that a boy's body had been washed ashore twenty miles down, and ten men, headed by Red George, went and brought it solemnly back to Pine-tree Gulch. There among the stumps of pine trees a grave was dug, and there, in the presence of the whole camp, White-faced Dick was laid to rest.

Pine-tree Gulch is a solitude now, the trees are growing again, and none would dream that it was once a busy scene of industry; but if the traveler searches among the pine trees he will find a stone with the words:

"Here lies White-faced Dick, who died to save Red George. 'What can a man do more than give his life for a friend?'"

The text was the suggestion of an ex-clergyman working as a miner in Pine-tree Gulch.

Red George worked no more at the diggings, but, after seeing the stone laid in its place, went east, and with what little money came to him when the common fund of the company was divided after the flood on the Yuba, bought a small farm, and settled down there; but to the end of his life he was never weary of telling those who would listen to it the story of Pine-tree Gulch.